LAST RESORT

Silver looked directly at Magbe. "In a few hours a missile will carry a bomb that will destroy all forms of life for one hundred miles in diameter. That's why we were taking your people to Alexandria. To get them out of harm's way. Now you're leading them to their death."

"She lies. There is no such weapon," said Benhaddou.

"There is. It's called a neutron bomb. It can destroy all forms of life. You don't have a chance if you stay in the desert."

Magbe turned to Benhaddou. "What do we do?"

Benhaddou looked at Silver. "She is lying. There's no such weapon. We continue with our plan. But first . . . I will kill Creighton."

Also by Bill Dolan

**AFRIKORPS
IRON HORSE
WHITE RHINO
SEA STALLION
LION MOUNTAIN**

Published by
HarperPaperbacks

ATTENTION: ORGANIZATIONS AND CORPORATIONS

Most HarperPaperbacks are available at special quantity discounts for bulk purchases for sales promotions, premiums, or fund-raising. For information, please call or write:
**Special Markets Department, HarperCollins Publishers,
10 East 53rd Street, New York, N.Y. 10022.
Telephone: (212) 207-7528. Fax: (212) 207-7222.**

BILL DOLAN
AFRIKORPS

COBRA CURSE

HarperPaperbacks
A Division of HarperCollinsPublishers

If you purchased this book without a cover, you should be aware that this book is stolen property. It was reported as "unsold and destroyed" to the publisher and neither the author nor the publisher has received any payment for this "stripped book."

This is a work of fiction. The characters, incidents, and dialogues are products of the author's imagination and are not to be construed as real. Any resemblance to actual events or persons, living or dead, is entirely coincidental.

HarperPaperbacks *A Division of* HarperCollins*Publishers*
10 East 53rd Street, New York, N.Y. 10022

Copyright © 1993 by HarperCollins*Publishers*
All rights reserved. No part of this book may be used or reproduced in any manner whatsoever without written permission of the publisher, except in the case of brief quotations embodied in critical articles and reviews. For information address HarperCollins*Publishers*, 10 East 53rd Street, New York, N.Y. 10022.

Cover illustration by Danilo

First printing: May 1993

Printed in the United States of America

HarperPaperbacks and colophon are trademarks of HarperCollins*Publishers*

❖10 9 8 7 6 5 4 3 2 1

For my friend Kahlil Johnson, known around the neighborhood as "C. J.," of Grand Forks, North Dakota.

And especially for my good friend and neighbor Gary Gardner.

Finally, I would like to thank my editor at HarperPaperbacks, Jessica Lichtenstein, for her terrific patience and help in the completion of the AfriKorps series.

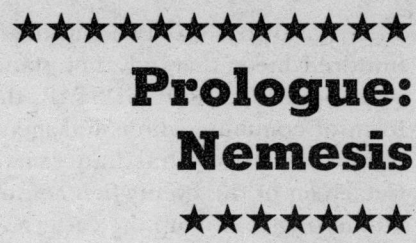

Prologue: Nemesis

★★★★★★★★

Eastern Quadrant. North Africa. A.D. 2177
1400.

Captain Reno Falken pushed back his floppy desert hat, revealing piercing blue eyes framed within a bronze face; a face that was now twisted into a mask of torment. He was walking through an outpost on the eastern edge of the East Quadrant now designated a "Green Zone," pacified and recovering from the hellish effects of tribal warfare and the recent defeat of the southern-based Marauder nation.

Or so he thought. From all appearances the war was still raging as he stepped through the front door of the communications center. The stench of dried blood stung his nostrils; the buzzing of flies filled the hot air, and he felt his stomach might give way any moment to the nausea consuming him.

"Damn," he whispered as he stepped over the mutilated body of an officer from the multinational force assigned to the outpost. He rolled the officer over and then froze, staring into the dead soldier's empty sockets.

He gripped his communicator attached to his harness and spoke quickly. "TC . . . you better get in here. I've found something you'll want to see."

The outpost was two hundred meters by two hundred meters, an advance station designed as a relay point for GROUNDSTAR, the most advanced form of communications linkage since the satellite communication that had existed prior to the Cataclysm of the twenty-first century. AfriKorps was attempting to link up the eastern African continent through the biospheres where a small percentage of certain governments had survived the century-long hell created by the greenhouse effect.

The outpost had ceased communication with AfriKorps HQ in what was once Morocco three days before. Leading the patrol was Major Abraham "TC" Creighton, a battle-hardened veteran of the Marauder campaign and of the final campaign to pacify the western United States prior to deployment to Africa. Creighton and Falken had grown up together and soldiered at the Vegas Biosphere in what was called DesFor—Desert Force—of the western United States. Creighton was tall, with deep brown eyes that narrowed to two burning slits when he stepped beside Falken.

Creighton didn't need more than a look to know what had happened to the MNF soldier. His throat was slit from ear to ear, but it was the fact his eyeballs were missing that sealed the identity of the murderer.

"That sonofabitch!" Creighton seethed. He switched his communicator to the On position. "Shona . . . get over to the commo building."

Shona arrived a few minutes later. He was tall, with rich ebony skin. A native of North Africa, he had miraculously survived the Cataclysm, living as a nomad in the desert. He had joined the AfriKorps force as an interpreter and soldier.

COBRA CURSE

When Shona saw the body he knew their nemesis had passed through the area. A nemesis that was his brother: Benhaddou.

The voice of a soldier broke over the communicator. "Major . . . we've got tread tracks moving east. There are four units." There was a pause. "From what I can see they're American built MBTs."

Creighton looked quickly at Falken. "Now we know what happened to the Riersgard patrol."

Captain Dale Riersgard had been on patrol for over two weeks when he suddenly quit reporting. Then the outpost quit reporting. The two facts were not lost on Creighton.

"Benhaddou must have penetrated their security and overpowered them and taken their equipment."

Falken nodded. "He's a crafty bastard. He could have learned how to operate the units and train others."

The three men knew the renegade Morocc was an intelligent and wily fighter. Now he was even more dangerous. He had in his control four armored units with weapons platforms capable of destroying any armored vehicle on earth, including the units commanded by Creighton.

1900.

His name was Benhaddou, and his lip curled upward with joy as he recalled the screams of the soldiers led by the white-skinned captain named Riersgard. Benhaddou had slowly peeled every inch of skin off the soldiers, forcing the young officer to watch until his turn came. With each soldier fresh information was revealed until he knew everything he and his band of renegade followers needed to know to operate the MBTs and their sophisticated weapons systems. He had taken three days, slowly and cruelly extracting information that could not be withheld under excruciating torture.

A year before his miraculous escape from prison at AfriKorps HQ, he had learned much about the AfriKorps: their language, their technology, and their tactics. Following his escape he wandered south to join the Marauders but was forced again east where he found those willing to follow him in his retaliatory trek.

His first realization was that he would need equipment, then he would travel farther east beyond the reach of AfriKorps and establish his own empire. He had heard of other biospheres in the eastern desert—in Egypt—where he was confident he could organize other followers into an army capable of standing firm against AfriKorps.

What he needed was the technology. The MBTs were the first step; now he needed to find those with the capability of duplicating the fighting machines.

There was such a place. He had captured a woman named Amina, a bronze-skinned Egyptian who knew of a man in the Cairo Biosphere who would aid him. She was traveling with her father, a diplomat from Cairo, en route to make contact with whatever governments he might find in the west. She said other legations had set out as well. They were dispersed like the sand in the wind, to find other surviving biospherans.

She said she did not know the name of the man in Cairo; that his only identity was a name she had heard whispered throughout her childhood while growing up: he was called the Hakama!

0600.

Creighton felt the fatigue gnawing at his system but continued to press forward. The eight MBTs in his patrol had pressed east through the darkness, locked onto the tread tracks in a desperate attempt to overtake the fleeing renegades. At sunrise he knew the chase was hopeless; there was too much distance between the two elements. He drew the patrol to a halt in the eastern desert where the earth seemed to open, revealing a deep canyon he figured was several thousand feet deep. The giant fissure was a result of the Cataclysm; subterranean movement had created an almost impassable obstacle.

"There's no chance of catching them, TC." Falken spoke from the lead vehicle, an IFV—infantry fighting vehicle—equipped with heavy machine guns and carrying twelve infantry soldiers.

"We could send for *Scorpion One*. The aircraft can cover more area than an MBT. And faster."

Reno shrugged. "Give the old man a call. But remember this: *Scorpion One* will be up against four AfriKorps MBTs, not a bunch of rusted out gas guzzlers like we saw down south."

Creighton gave that some thought. Reno was right. The match wouldn't be even, especially if Benhaddou knew how to operate the TIRT heat-seeking missiles. "Maybe you're right."

Before Reno could respond a familiar voice broke over another channel.

Colonel Thomas Clayton, commander of

AfriKorps, ordered, "Break off pursuit and return to headquarters. Report immediately upon arrival."

Sergeant Steve Puhaly, the muscular gunner, sat below Creighton in the MBT they called Ribald's Chariot. He spit absently at the instrument console that controlled the MBTs massive weapons system. "Do we ignore the message?"

TC shook his head. "Negative. There'll be another time." He pressed the communicator. "All units . . . return to HQ. Reno, take the point. Move at Full Fast Forward."

The units swung around and moved in a long line, retracing their tracks while thundering toward the west.

On the opposite side of the deep fissure, from behind an outcropping of boulders, Benhaddou studied the armored column through his field binoculars. He grinned as he saw the pursuit breaking off; relief flooded through him. He wasn't yet prepared for a confrontation with experienced AfriKorps soldiers. That would come later, when he was ready.

First, he had to reach Cairo.

★★★★★★★★★★★★★

PART ONE: THE HAKAMA

★★★★★★★★

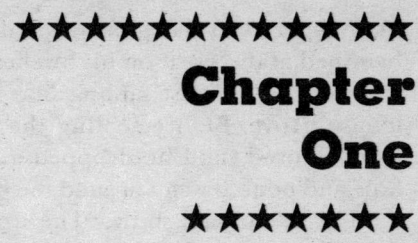

Chapter One

★★★★★★★★

Base Camp One. AfriKorps HQ.

Hamp Florens was an agronomist; a quiet man with a cherubic face that seemed perpetually burned from hours in the sun despite his wearing a floppy hat that seemed to protect only his balding head. Hamp was a man who could raise cotton in the desert, or grow fruit trees on the side of rocky mountains. He was, indeed, a man with a green thumb.

Hamp was the descendant of an agronomist; as he was growing up in the Vegas Biosphere the only gardens he ever saw were hidden from the sun, lighted by artificial, refracting light and moistened by water created within the world of the biosphere.

The first time he stepped into the sunlight he understood the power of the sun. Though it was too powerful at that time, he knew eventually the intensity would diminish, as the ozone layer had nearly repaired itself.

He was a survivor of the Cataclysm. Like others, he understood the importance of the earth and its natural biomes when he stepped from the artificial world of the biosphere into the regenerating world of an earth environment.

Another survivor was Dr. Said Qannatar, who was

much shorter with thick glasses and a drooping mustache; he wiped at the sweat on his forehead while watching Hamp plant the last sapling in a freshly cultivated lemon grove. Before sealing the sapling with the loam-colored sand he dropped a tiny pill into the hole and poured water around the base of the roots.

"There," he said softly. "The tree should begin a daily growth rate of twenty-five percent and reach maturity within two months."

"Incredible." Said breathed heavily. "I have never seen such amazing growth. How is this done?"

Hamp patted a pouch containing the seeds. "We have a means of energizing the plant growth through a discovery provided us by distant friends of our planet."

Said looked at him strangely. He did not understand, and Hamp was certain that he never could understand the fact that in recent months the AfriKorps had encountered a colony of aliens who arrived in South Africa just after the beginning of the Cataclysm, bringing with them technology beyond human understanding.

Hamp simply responded, "In a few months you'll have fresh lemons and other vegetation. Trees will again flourish. Birds will return."

"Birds? Where will you find birds?"

"From the biospheres in America. Aviaries were established in both the desert biomes and the rain forest biomes by my government before Cataclysm. And other countries as well."

"Birds. Amazing."

The two men stood, and Hamp could see as Said's eyes swept the new orchard that he was amazed—and proud. Trees planted the day before were taller than those planted this day; shorter than those planted several days before.

Hamp wiped his hands on his shirt and started toward the truck that was his mobile agriculture center when he saw a rooster tail rising above the sand. He knew immediately it was a column of AfriKorps MBTs returning from patrol to the east.

The distinct signature of the AfriKorps MBT was like no other armored unit in the modern world. There was a rooster tail, but no sign of the tank. The tank was wrapped by its own stealth-creating computer system, which allowed the unit literally to disappear within the cloud of dust.

The MBT rolled to a whirring stop and the upper cupola opened. Major Abraham "TC" Creighton's head popped through the open hatch. He removed his helmet, a combination sighting and communication unit capable of many tasks including fire control and missile launch. With a wink of his eye he could fire all the weapons at a target locked into the sighting mechanism of the helmet.

"Don't you listen to your commo unit?" asked Creighton.

Hamp grinned. "I hate the bloody communicators. I'm a farmer, not a soldier."

TC laughed. "Colonel Clayton wants you back at headquarters. He asked me to swing by on my way back to bivouac."

Hamp waved at him and turned, calling over his shoulder, "Tell him I'll be there when I can."

The MBT rolled away, and Hamp couldn't help but wonder why Clayton would want him.

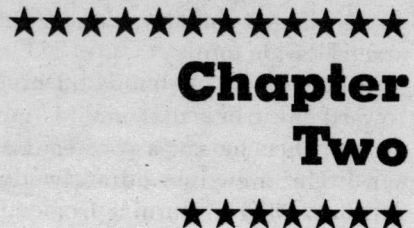

Chapter Two

★★★★★★★

1300.

Colonel Thomas Clayton was tall and powerfully built; his graying hair flowed back over his ears, giving him a distinguished look. Only the hardness of his mouth and the sharpness of his eyes set him apart from the others in the command center of AfriKorps HQ. The others in the room were diplomats and scientists, including Hamp Florens and Dr. Qannatar.

Major Abe Creighton stood along the wall, his arms folded as he watched the AfriKorps commander turn on a hologram. A map of east Africa suddenly materialized in the air. Clayton reached into the air and touched a spot along the northern coast.

"This is Alexandria. Diplomatic relations have been established, and the inhabitants are interested in establishing GROUNDSTAR hookup with the outside world. Like most biospheres, their communications have been limited to short-range output. Our final mission in this overall operation is to establish rail linkage between our location and Alexandria, then swing south to this point."

He was touching the Cairo Biosphere.

Clayton continued. "The Iron Horse unit will move east to Alexandria under a protective umbrella of four MBTs. Once that service has been established the unit will swing south to Cairo. The rail link should be complete by tomorrow. Mr. Derider's track-laying crew is closing in on Alexandria at this time."

"Why so much protection for the GROUNDSTAR personnel? I thought the Marauders were defeated and all the hostile nomads pacified," asked one of the scientists.

"We've reason to believe there's a renegade element operating to the east." He nodded at Creighton. "A patrol returned this morning with a disturbing report. One of our GROUNDSTAR outposts was destroyed and all personnel killed. All signs indicate they were attacked by armored units of American design. In all likelihood the renegades are led by our old nemesis Benhaddou."

This didn't seem to register with the scientists. Clayton tried to clarify. "You may recall the Riersgard patrol has been overdue for some time. We have assessed the situation and concluded they were compromised. If that's the case, the renegades are roaming around out there with some pretty hefty firepower. All units are on alert for that possibility."

"Are you certain it was Benhaddou?" asked Hamp. He had encountered the man before, nearly losing his life to his treachery.

"No question. Major Creighton personally made the identification."

A murmur rolled through the room. There was no doubting the implication. There was no secret of the hatred felt toward Benhaddou by Creighton and all the troops of AfriKorps.

"How was contact established with Alexandria?" asked another scientist.

"Through *Sea Stallion*." He was referring to the solar-powered attack hovercraft developed by the young but ambitious new U.S. navy. "Captain Bruce Wills reached Alexandria two days ago. He was accompanied by Roman Standish and an envoy from several European nations informing their biosphere government that the train was approaching their location. The Egyptians are more than willing to become a new member of the growing world community. Unlike our country, they have maintained limited contact with one another over the duration of the Cataclysm. It's our understanding that Cairo has dispatched several legations . . . only one has succeeded in getting through to Alexandria."

It was common knowledge that the new world community was rapidly pulling itself back together since the cessation of the Cataclysm. Governments—and a limited number of personnel—had survived the horror by living inside giant glasslike biospheres capable of withstanding the ravages of the Cataclysm and the outside assault from humans left to fend for themselves. Now that the horror was over, the world was starting to repair its diplomatic ties.

Clayton pointed at Hamp. "Roman Standish has sent a message. He wants Hamp to join the patrol to Alexandria, bringing with him whatever is necessary to begin agricultural operations."

Hamp didn't look pleased. "My goodness, Thomas. That will be quite impossible."

Clayton chuckled. "My goodness, Hamp—that is an order. Pack up your plants and get ready to roll when Major Creighton gives you the word. You've more greenery to plant."

"What about my work here, Colonel?"

"That can take care of itself. You have people you can depend on to maintain this operation. You're needed in Alexandria. Afterward, you'll go to Cairo."

"Cairo!" Hamp said the word as though swallowing hot lead.

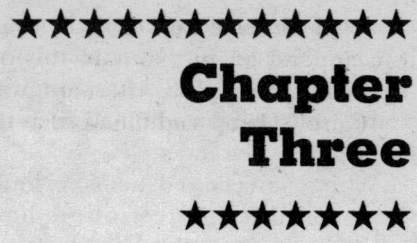

Chapter Three

★★★★★★★★

Captain Silver Allenbey-Creighton was beautiful; to Creighton her blond hair and blue eyes seemed joined as he walked through the field hospital. She knew there was something bothering him. She thought she knew the answer.

It had been three days since his return from the desert where the destroyed outpost had been discovered. He had said nothing to her about Benhaddou. She had once been the African's victim, and was miraculously brought back to life by a miracle given to earth by the arrival of the Progenitor, an alien being that offered to the earth the ability to regenerate life through a simple blood sample. She had been literally reborn; so was Falken, who had suffered mortal injuries in the southern area of Marauderland.

The blood sample used to regenerate her life had been drawn prior to her death, therefore she could not recall the ravage she suffered at the hands of Benhaddou in the desert only weeks after her arrival in North Africa.

She was glad. Abe Creighton never discussed the incident and it was best left with no explanation.

But now there were other matters to discuss. Matters of a personal nature.

Recent tests had confirmed a suspicion that only a woman can feel. She felt radiant as she watched him approach along the aisle, stopping occasionally to speak with a soldier who had been injured during the war with the Marauders.

When he reached her she took his hand, and they walked to the rear of the hospital, where she led him out into the hot afternoon sun. The sky was brilliant; only a few clouds marred an otherwise perfect setting.

"When are you leaving?" she asked.

He shrugged. "I think tomorrow morning. Departure will be determined by the crew on the train. The chief engineer should have his crew ready by midnight. We'll load up and drop off four MBTs with the GROUNDSTAR crew, then push on to Alexandria. We should arrive there in about twelve hours."

She knew the Iron Horse, as the supersonic train was called, would get the personnel and equipment to the end of the track—six hundred miles to the east—in record time.

The train was a combination bullet train and fighting platform with an array of weaponry that made it virtually invincible. Only the human element needed protection, the road gang that lay the bed the train traveled over.

"How long will you be gone?"

"A month. Maybe longer. Maybe less."

"Is there danger?"

He shook his head. "Nothing to be concerned about."

She suddenly took on a glow. "There's something I want you to know before you leave."

He looked at her long and intently. He felt her fingers lace through his.

"What?"

"We're going to have a baby."

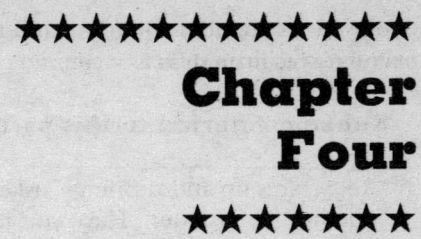

Chapter Four

0700.

Debarkation of the expedition began at what was called the roundhouse, the maintenance center where the train was based. The chief engineer, Nicholas Ruhland, was a man who regarded his train as more than a technological wonder; to him the train was almost human. The special computer system allowed him audio communication, thus making the operation more personal and simple. The computer could scan its systems and report any malfunctions or potential problem areas.

Creighton found Ruhland at the control panel in the lead engine; an engine similar to the rear engine. The train could operate on either the front or aft engine along a roadbed impregnated with a computerized rail system with antitampering devices. Should a terrorist tamper with the system, an immediate electrical charge would be pulsed by the central control.

The weapons were SMART missiles capable of flying a pattern, searching out targets of definitive shape to destroy or ignore them, then return to the train, where the missile could be recovered for use at another time. Heavy armor-piercing guns were deployed throughout the train, and there were other necessary facilities such as a commo car and a hospital car.

Ruhland referred to this particular train as "Marge."

"All systems up and running?" asked Creighton.

"Purring like a kitten. Have you loaded your men and equipment?"

Creighton nodded. "The medical crew will arrive in a few minutes, then we can push off."

"Medical crew? Are you expecting trouble?"

Creighton shook his head. "Negative. But the old man wants us to bring along a medical crew. There's no guarantee the people in Alexandria have avoided disease since the Cataclysm. It's just a precaution."

"And the GROUNDSTAR crew? Are they aboard?"

"Loaded and ready to roll."

"We'll be ready."

Creighton left and went four cars down the line where his squadron of MBTs was loading into dozens of cars. The heavy 120 mm barrels had been removed to provide more room. Since the trip would last little more than three hours, there was no need for the men and women of the patrol to use the quarters provided in each car. The troops would stay with their equipment.

Creighton found Puhaly and the driver, Corporal Fergus Felot, sitting in the open door of the car. Captain Mike Armbrust, the commander of Panther squadron, was standing on the ground talking to the men.

Armbrust saluted; Puhaly and Felot merely nodded

at Creighton.

"Ready to get ballistic?" asked Creighton.

Armbrust shook his head. "Are you sure this crate can hold up at supersonic?"

Creighton laughed. "We won't be supersonic. But we'll be moving out. The engineer plans on staying at approximately 200 miles per hour."

Puhaly whistled. "Man, that's traveling."

"That's a helluva improvement over the earlier model," added Armbrust.

"Yeah. We're bringing modern technology to Africa."

"Shit." replied Felot. "I'd rather be taking Ribald's Chariot back to Vegas. I'm sick of this continent, TC. When are we going back to the United States?"

Creighton sat in the door; he was looking at the stars. The thought of becoming a father had forced himself to ask that same question. "The old man said as soon as this operation is over the initial elements will be going back. Those who want to stay will be assigned to units in the pacified areas. There's no combat left, but there's still a training agenda."

Puhaly spoke up. "Then I'm staying. I ain't going back to be no damn farmer. I've gotten to like the place. Besides, if Fergus is back in DesFor, I'd prefer to keep an ocean between us. I've been smelling his damn feet for too many years."

The others laughed, but Creighton looked down the line. He could see the medical unit was nearly loaded.

Just as Creighton turned back to the others, a single figure walked quickly from the bus that carried the medical personnel from the hospital.

Captain Silver Allenbey-Creighton walked hurriedly up the loading ramp and disappeared inside the medical unit's car.

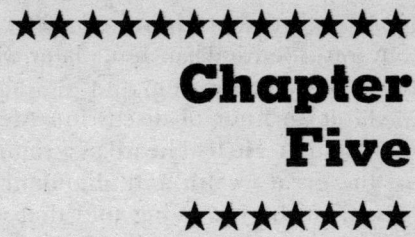
Chapter Five

★★★★★★★★

Benhaddou had learned that power was something that was given, not taken. To seize power meant there would be too many to distrust. This he had learned from Amina. She had surrendered herself to him in order to survive. She saw in him the chance to live.

That was the power he had over her. The same power he would soon exercise over the hundreds of nomadic tribesmen assembled in the desert three hundred miles east of the fissure where he had eluded the AfriKorps. He was fifty kilometers from Cairo, and his plan was unfolding perfectly.

The nomads had watched with wide eyes as the small armored column rolled into their village located on the edge of an oasis. Through Amina he had talked with the man who was the leader of the nomads, an old man who wore nothing but a loincloth. The others were dressed similarly, including the women and children. They carried sharpened sticks for weapons, which they lowered upon seeing the destructive weapons carried by the renegades.

A wise choice, thought Benhaddou. He had given the nomads a demonstration of the MBTs firepower, then sent Amina as his envoy. Benhaddou's tanks were parked three hundred meters from the oasis. She returned half an hour later with the old man, who was called Afez.

After an hour of discussion Afez agreed to join Benhaddou. He had heard as a young man the stories of the great wealth and abundance of food in the east. Now he was being told that wealth was his to share. All he had to do was supply Benhaddou with the men to help form his army. An army that would be trained in the use of modern weapons.

Benhaddou envisioned himself marching at the lead of a great nomadic army. With great numbers—and the four MBTs—he could force the people in the Cairo Biosphere to join his army. Join or die.

He knew the Cairo biosphere had weapons, tanks, though not of the caliber of the ones he had captured from the Americans. But they were formidable against an equal army. An army that lived farther to the east, where the combined forces could destroy a foe and render more weapons to his army.

He had learned long ago that he could not outfight the AfriKorps. He might elude them, growing stronger in numbers, then become diplomatic, joining their international community after having founded his personal kingdom.

Benhaddou gave Afez his instructions. "You will follow our line of march to Cairo. We must go ahead in order to make contact with other friends who will join our forces."

Afez understood. "You will leave one of the giant fighting turtles to give us protection?"

Benhaddou understood. "Yes. The fighting turtles are called tanks. One will stay with your people. You must obey the orders of the man in charge of the tank. Bring as much food and water as you can carry. The journey must take no longer than three days."

"That is a great distance to travel in three days. Many will die."

"Those who survive will find great abundance waiting."

Afez nodded, then stood. "When will you leave?"

"Tonight." Benhaddou watched the old man walk back to the village. To Amina he said, "This man you call the Hakama. He can be trusted?"

"He can."

"And he will be able to get others to join us. Others with the knowledge to be of assistance?"

She looked toward the village. "These people are ignorant and have no knowledge of the skills you need. The Hakama will have followers who will understand the technology you are bringing. The soldiers in the Cairo biosphere will not resist once they see how your weapons are superior. The Hakama will know which engineers you'll need to manufacture more weapons similar to these."

"Do you think he will join us?"

There was the look of assurance on her face. "He will join us. He has waited a long time for someone like you."

Benhaddou's eyes narrowed. Again he asked, "Can he be trusted?"

She smiled. "Is that important?"

Benhaddou laughed. "No. It is not important. We will only need him for a short time."

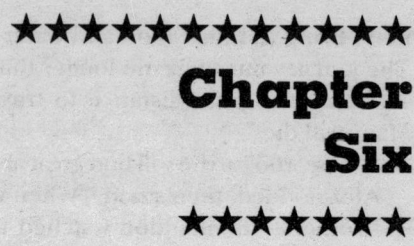
Chapter Six

Alexandria Biosphere.

Roman Standish had remained at the Alexandria biosphere after the departure of *Sea Stallion*. He solely represented the AfriKorps diplomatic delegation and found the duty rather amusing.

It reminded him of when he was a teacher in the Vegas biosphere and his students thirsted for information. The Egyptians were just as thirsty. They knew very little of what had happened in the world beyond their glass walls since the Cataclysm.

"How many European biospheres survived?" asked a young man.

"Almost all survived, with only a few being either penetrated by those left on the outside . . . or from insurrection on the inside."

"Insurrection?" asked another.

Roman grew serious. "Not all humans selected for the biospheres were capable of withstanding the psychological stress of watching the Cataclysm unfold. There were a few instances where insanity prevailed. This caused destruction."

"How many on earth survived the Cataclysm?"

"You mean of those selected to go into biospheres. There were two thousand biospheres. Each biosphere had an average population of twenty-eight hundred. To our knowledge approximately forty biospheres did not survive the Cataclysm." He figured quickly. "With growth rate management that's approximately five million survivors."

A hush fell over the group. They were sitting in the sand outside the biosphere. The sky was clear, and Roman, wearing his toga and with his long silver hair tied in a ponytail, was the appearance of Socrates holding class before his students.

"What of those who survived the Cataclysm outside the biospheres?" asked a young woman.

"What we called the hostiles. In America, miraculously, there were several hundred thousand survivors throughout the nation. Most were in the mountain and desert regions, where there was shelter and limited wildlife. The forested regions of the south and east were destroyed by the Cataclysm."

"What did your government do once the Cataclysm had ended?"

"We sent out an armored unit from the capital, Biosphere One. The unit was commanded by the man who is now president of our country. His name is Woolford Dawson. He and his men were very courageous. They made contact with European governments in France, Germany, and Spain. We now communicate regularly through a communication system called GROUNDSTAR."

"Not as sophisticated as satellite communication was," he was reminded.

"No. But there are no missiles to launch satellites. Hopefully there never will be such devices. They can be used improperly."

"Yes. We know. Before the Cataclysm the earth's

governments used missiles with great destructive power."

Quite so, thought Roman. Which was why before the Cataclysm all the governments of the world agreed under the Prometheus Project to destroy all weaponry that might fall into the hands of those left on the outside by the biospherans.

Vast armies of tanks were destroyed; battleships and great aircraft carriers were scuttled at sea. Missiles were dismantled for self-preservation. What had taken centuries to develop was destroyed in order to save the privileged few who were descendants of the very development of mass destruction.

"How did you settle your country? The nomads surrounding our biospheres were savages. Our soldiers fought bravely, but now they are afraid."

"We sent our trained soldiers into the field to pacify the hostiles." There was a look of sadness on his face.

The woman asked, "How did you achieve this pacification?"

Roman answered in a soft voice, "Mainly through submission. Our technology is far superior to yours."

"You killed them?"

"Yes, but not all of them. Granted, they were very violent. Very unpredictable. Those who were captured were brought into camps, given training, and then taken to small farms where they presently live, trying to help rebuild our nation."

"Then you didn't slaughter them?" asked an older man.

"Of course not. Many were killed but they were unwilling to surrender. We have a world to rebuild. Sometimes extreme measures are warranted in light of the overall objective. That objective is to civilize the earth once again."

"What about religion?" asked the old man.

"What of it?"

"What religion does your people practice?"

Roman shrugged. He had not given religion much thought in his life, except from its historical perspective. From what he knew, religion might have killed more humans throughout time than the Cataclysm.

"Our nation does not practice any particular religion. There are those who are religious, a tradition passed down through the years in various biospheres. The entire range, including a few sects of your Islam."

"Do you believe in God?" asked the old man.

Roman shrugged. "I don't know."

This sent a murmur through the group. The old man stood and quietly walked away.

"Who is that man?" asked Roman.

The woman answered, "He is Anwar el-Riad."

"What is his function?'

"He is a mullah."

The old man went to his room, where he sat and read the Koran. After an hour he went to the communications center and sent a message to a young man he had met only through the radio equipment in the biosphere.

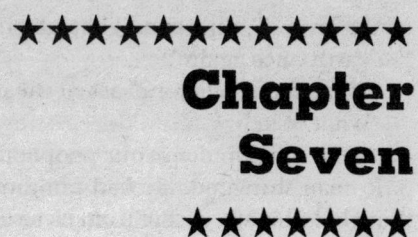

Chapter Seven

Cairo Biosphere.

At sunrise the muezzin, the crier to the faithful, stood at the upper level of the giant Biosphere, his words spoken over a loudspeaker that carried his voice to every room in the complex.

> *God is most great. I testify there is no God but Allah. Muhammad is God's Apostle. Come to prayer, come to success. God is most great.*

In one of the rooms, near the desert biome, five men sat in a row with hundreds of others, their lips moving, yet there were no words. In their minds they repeated over and over the words their ancestors had spoken for thousands of years; words of the faithful to Islam. Only one of the men knew the true dedication of the other four; they did not know his identity but knew he existed. This they had been assured through their fathers and grandfathers for over a hundred years.

They had been born with purpose.

With discipline and reverence the inhabitants had faithfully spread their prayer rugs and prayed to the east; prayed to the one spirit they believed would

COBRA CURSE

someday erase the yellow gas from the sky and return the green foliage to the earth.

The Cataclysm had destroyed earth, and in many nations the religion of entire societies was destroyed. But not in Egypt; not in the land of the Pharaohs, who once worshiped idols. Islam had been protected from the outset of the Cataclysm, giving the "specials" selected to ride out the natural catastrophe more than a scientific hope: they were given spiritual hope.

Miraculously, regeneration was occurring. Outside, water was receding from the flooded banks of the Nile; grass could be seen growing in soil that was once putrid with poison. The sky was blue, the sun hot but not all-consuming. The hundred-year nightmare appeared to be at an end.

To the five young men kneeling in prayer, it was the sign their fathers and grandfathers had predicted would come: the day of atonement within the biosphere for the sins committed against their religion, and the beginning of atonement for the infidels beyond the biosphere who had created this horror against the people of Islam.

Magbe Nihra carried the only sign that would signal the others his true identity, and with that the knowledge that the moment had come.

Magbe was sapling tall, lean, and wore a dark mustache over lips that never seemed to move; his long hair, cut short on top but long and ponytailed in the back, framed bronze features that appeared carved from granite. There was only softness in his voice; what few words he spoke were well chosen and always with purpose.

When the prayer session ended he returned to his

quarters. The moment he entered, he knew he was not alone. There was the distinct feeling of another's presence.

The door to the bathroom opened and a lithe figure walked toward him. He felt himself grow excited. "Amina."

She stepped into his arms and kissed him long and hungrily. Automatically they fell onto the bed, biting and kissing with a passion neither could control. She quickly guided him inside her and felt his manhood pulsating in a way she had never known from him. They had been lovers since their youth; she was the only one with whom he had confided his secret.

When finished, he struggled to his feet. As the wave of passion subsided he suddenly exclaimed, "I thought you were dead."

She explained what had happened. "The expedition my father was taking to the west was attacked by a band of renegades led by a man named Benhaddou. My father was killed. Benhaddou made me his slave. I became his confidante in order to survive."

"Where is he now?"

"He is west of here. He has a small contingency of armor and a large following of nomads. His strength grows every day."

Magbe thought of the reports from Alexandria. "There are other foreigners in Alexandria. A European and American force called AfriKorps."

She looked startled. "AfriKorps. Those are the soldiers Benhaddou despises. He has captured several of their tanks."

This information dramatically caught Magbe's

attention. "Tell me about the tanks. Are they like ours?"

She shook her head as she ran a finger along his stomach. "No. They are more advanced."

Magbe looked up. "Then the reports from Alexandria are true." There was a gleam in his eye.

"I know what you're thinking. You plan to overpower Benhaddou and use his equipment against the AfriKorps. That might not be wise. He's very treacherous."

"It's that treachery that makes him predictable." Then he thought of something. "Why did he let you come here?"

"He knows I have nowhere to go. He wants you to join forces with him."

"Why should he want me?" There was suspicion in his voice.

"I told him about you. That you have hundreds of secret followers in the Egyptian biospheres. He knows that would be an easier way to victory than fighting all the military forces."

Magbe thought about the communication he had received earlier from Alexandria. "The stars are starting to align. The moment has come. But we must be careful. We have AfriKorps on one side . . . and Benhaddou on the other."

"What can I do to help?"

Magbe sat at his desk and quickly wrote four messages. Each message said the same:

> *The Nile rises from death and the moon sits staring in shame;*
> *The Cobra crawls from the darkness and waits on the bank;*

*Fear not the Nile, nor the Moon, nor the Cobra:
Faith will protect and guide.*

"Deliver these messages, then return to Benhaddou."
He explained what she was to tell the renegade warrior.

Chapter Eight

★★★★★★★★

1900.

The messages were delivered that afternoon, and the four young men anxiously awaited the hour they would meet the man their forefathers had promised would one day rise and give a new leadership to the Moslem survivors of the Cataclysm.

They had called him the *Hakama*—the ruler— and he would be identified by the sign of the Cobra!

Abu Abdel walked quietly but carefully to the main entrance of the biosphere. He traveled south through the moonlit night until he reached a location five kilometers south of what had once been the capital of Egypt. When he saw the silhouette of the pyramid framed against the moonlight he knew his journey had not ended; rather, the journey had begun.

The Pyramids of Saqqâra had withstood the ravages of the Cataclysm as they had withstood the thousands of years of sandstorms that had historically occurred in the desert country.

Abu was twenty-four, short and muscular. He moved quickly across the sand for nearly an hour. He was not surprised that his tracks eventually joined four other sets of tracks in the sand, forming one trail that led to the base of the pyramid.

Abu stopped as he saw four lights from flashlights shining at the base of the pyramid. He approached without fear.

Magbe sat in the middle of a circle. He motioned Abu to take his place.

Abu sat in the circle beside three others he had known since childhood but never suspected they were a part of this secret society.

Ali Bakar sat at his left, a heavyset young man of Abu's age. Khalil Jabour sat to his right, a thin but determined-looking young man. Across the circle sat another he recognized, Semir Zeina, very short, with flaming eyes.

When they were all gathered Magbe turned and faced Mecca, leading them in prayer. When prayer was complete, he motioned them to his side.

"Observe, faithful followers, the sign you have waited to see." He loosened his ponytail and spread the hair from his scalp at the base of his neck. The four gasped as they shined their lights.

A coiled cobra rose from where the hairline began and spread onto the back of his head.

"*Alla—akhbar!*" whispered the four in soft murmuring tones.

The five discussed their plans in meticulous detail, with Magbe doing most of the talking. He explained each person's role in the cleansing process that would begin soon and lead to the restoration of Islamic rule.

"What you propose will require much weaponry," Abu pointed out. He knew there was a strong internal security contingent inside the biosphere. He was an officer in the limited military force that guarded the biosphere.

"The weaponry will soon be at our disposal," replied Magbe.

"From where?" asked Semir. "Do we have weapons cached in the desert?"

Magbe smiled slowly. "No. There is no cache. But there is a foreign military force en route from the west. They are called AfriKorps."

"How do you know this?" asked Khalil.

"Remember the name of the mullah our father's spoke of?"

"Anwar el-Riad," they said in unison.

"Yes. Anwar el-Riad. He sent me a message. Look."

Magbe reached into his shirt and removed a map. He spread the map onto the sand. In the beam of the flashlights they saw a map of Africa. From the northernmost point of Africa a red line stretched south to the tip, to the land once called South Africa.

"Nearly two years ago a multinational force composed of Americans and Europeans was sent to Africa to pacify the continent. There was a large army to the south—called Marauders—who were marching up the continent with designs on the farmland of Europe. The force was called AfriKorps. They recently defeated the Marauders and have returned to their base in what was once Morocco." He tapped the map.

"They are coming here?" asked Abu.

Magbe nodded. "A sea vessel has arrived at the Alexandria biosphere. Two squadrons of sophisticated armor are sweeping from the west along the coast.

Diplomatic relations have been established. Anwar el-Riad said AfriKorps has the most advanced technological weapons ever known to the world. Armored tanks that can become virtually invisible and are powered by the sun. Missiles of such destructive power that nothing can stop the AfriKorps."

"How can we defeat such a force?" asked Semir incredulously.

An evil smile stretched across Magbe's mouth. He informed them of Benhaddou. Then he added, "We will destroy them all through the way of the cobra. The cobra hides from its enemy, then moves closer, never revealing its presence. When it's victim is unaware . . . it strikes!" His hand flashed at Semir with the speed of the deadly reptile.

Semir jerked back instinctively. "We make Benhaddou think we are his allies," he said flatly. "All the while we learn their technology. When we are prepared, we strike!"

"Yes. But first we must capture the Cairo Biosphere."

"How do we do that?"

Magbe explained his plan. Then he added, "We must contact all of the followers you have recruited over the years. Your fathers gave you the names of those we can trust in Cairo. It is time they were told to rise in the name of Allah."

"We have no weapons. The governor still has a strong force of soldiers."

"We don't need weapons. We have something else."

"What?"

Magbe carefully explained his plan, then he reminded them, "Remember: it is important for our followers to do as I've instructed. They must store the necessary supplies they will need."

Semir grinned. "They will never know what's happening."

★★★★★★★★★★★★★
Chapter Nine
★★★★★★★

The wind blew hot over the desert, giving not relief but torturing the party of engineers sent to survey an oasis west of Cairo. A carpet of stars stretched endlessly overhead wherever the team of surveyors looked. They slept in the open, sweating on their blankets, listening to the sounds of the desert carried on the wind.

One of the engineers, a young man named Hassan heard a scraping sound and sat up quickly. He couldn't see through the darkness, but he could feel the presence of something. A creature? A human?

Beside him Hafez, an older man, chuckled. "The night speaks to you, Hassan. Don't be afraid. There is only the sand and the wind. Nothing lives in the desert since the Cataclysm. Even the desert barely survived." He rolled over and tried to sleep. That was when he heard the distinctive sound again.

"The vultures survived."

"Vultures! Hah!" He hawked and spat into the sand. "Vultures are not night creatures."

"There are other night creatures. Cobras. Reptiles of such great length they can swallow a whole man."

Again the old man spat. "You've listened to too many tales. There is nothing out here but the desert. The stars. And no women."

He laughed again as Hassan walked away from the campfire.

Hassan stepped into the darkness to relieve himself when there was the sudden ear-cracking sound of gunfire.

He turned to the camp and saw men racing toward the survey crew, firing their weapons like demons.

At the lead of the men was a tall black man who wore a turban around his head.

Screams filled the night.

The few soldiers assigned to guard the crew were quickly dispatched. Then Hassan saw the first of the tanks appear. Then another. Tanks of a design he had never seen before.

Machine-gun fire drew a red tongue of flame through the night, joining the fleeing soldiers to the charging tanks. Two men were simultaneously lifted from their feet and pushed forward on their toes, appearing to be pulling the tank. Only when the gunner behind the coaxial machine gun shifted his field of fire to another group of men did the two fall to the sand.

The tall man with the turban raced toward Hafez, who could only stand there and watch. The moment Benhaddou fired a bullet into the old man's brain, Hafez's eyes closed to the horror. He pitched backward and lay silent.

Benhaddou motioned toward the darkness. From beyond the dunes there appeared dozens of ghoulish figures that hurried to the fallen bodies. Like vultures of the desert they quickly stripped the dead of their clothing.

"Nomads," Hassan hissed. He had heard stories of the desert wanderers, survivors of the Cataclysm. The stories he had heard as a boy turned his blood to jelly. Now he understood. They slit the throats of the wounded with no compassion. Slowly the screams receded, as one by one the survivors of the party were systematically executed.

Carefully, like a snake slithering backward, Hassan inched his way down the crest of the dune into the shadows. He took a few seconds to catch his breath, then whispered softly, "Allah be merciful."

Then he turned and started to run with all his strength. He ran east, toward Cairo.

Chapter Ten

Creighton's squadron had been bivouaced outside the Alexandria Biosphere for three days when he discovered his wife had accompanied the patrol. He was livid when he walked into the hospital tent and found her taking blood samples from a group of children.

"Why are you here?" he asked flatly.

She continued drawing blood from a young boy's arm. She seemed to be ignoring Creighton, knowing that was the best policy at the moment.

"Roman reported a disease before we departed Base Camp One. I'm a hematologist. Colonel Clayton thought it best if I accompany the patrol." Her voice was calm and this only added to Creighton's anger.

"I thought you had learned your lesson. This is a soldier's patrol, not a medical patrol."

"I'm a captain . . . Major. Which means I'm also a soldier." She was dressed in standard AfriKorps desert shorts, short-sleeve blouse, and kepi, a hat reminiscent of the old French Foreign Legion uniforms.

"Clayton. I should have known. That bastard's always interfering in my private affairs."

"He's your father. He has the right."

"A father I've never known. And look what happened the last time. Or have you forgotten?"

"Of course I've forgotten. When the Progenitor re-created my body from a blood sample drawn on my arrival in Africa, everything that followed is forgotten."

"It's not forgotten to me, dammit! I lived through the pain. I had to suffer. I don't want that again."

"Benhaddou won't bother me. You think he's farther to the south. I won't be going south, I promise."

"You're damned right you won't be going south. You're going west."

Abe Creighton turned and stormed out of the hospital. Silver took the blood samples and went to a hemascope, designed to give an instant evaluation of the samples.

What she saw made her eyes widen. She had seen the same image in textbooks during her medical training. The blood revealed a virus that attacked the immune system. The virus, labeled type H204, was similar to the HIV-type virus that had ravaged the twentieth century before a cure was found.

She quickly examined this particular child's medical records. The child was the daughter of a scientist who had made the perilous trip from the Cairo Biosphere to help establish a governing body for Egypt now that reconstruction could begin. The child, her father and mother, were all dead. They had died within hours of reaching Alexandria.

Silver had been warned before leaving the United States she might encounter diseases that had not been seen in the United States since the Cataclysm. Confinement in the biospheres for more than a century had protected the survivors from all disease that rampaged outside. Now that the survivors were becoming exposed to the outside, it was expected their immune systems would not tolerate even the slightest viral attack. In this case there was no threat if they were treated within hours of the appearance of symptoms. This made her realize something else as well: she wouldn't be able to keep her promise to her husband.

She would have to go to Cairo. To treat the virus.

Chapter Eleven

Magbe rose from his prayer rug and went to a cabinet secreted in the wall. Inside the cabinet was a metal container. He carefully opened the container and observed the four flasks sealed with rubber stoppers. He carefully removed one flask and held it to the light. The flask held less liquid than the other three. He knew why: he had carefully doctored the drinking water of a man he despised. The man had been sent to Alexandria with his family. And the message from Anwar el-Riad confirmed that the entire family was now dead.

Soon, others would be dead. But only those selected by Magbe.

Suddenly the door flew open. Abu entered with a face filled with fright.

"Magbe, there are soldiers approaching."

Magbe hurried past Abu and stood at the railing. Below, hundreds of men and women were assembled. A young man seemed to be at the center of attention. Magbe recognized him as a young engineer who had recently been directed to lead a party to the western region in search of fertile territory that could be repopulated by inhabitants of the biosphere.

"I've never seen such ferocious looking people. We

were attacked by a tank that appeared out of nowhere."

"What of the others?' asked Thalmus, the governor of the biosphere.

"Dead. All dead."

"How did you escape?"

"I escaped under cover of darkness."

"How far are they from here?"

"Twenty kilometers."

Magbe pushed his way through the crowd. He was a man who knew opportunity when he saw it. That which frightened the others gave him hope.

"What are you planning to do, Governor?" Magbe demanded.

"To approach them peacefully."

"Peacefully. That's absurd. They have already slaughtered our people. You cannot negotiate with murderers."

Thalmus walked to Magbe, stopping close enough to taste his breath. "What do you suggest? We have no army that can defeat such a force."

"There are those who can defend us. In Alexandria. They move across the desert like lightning."

Thalmus heard the grumbling of the others. "As you wish. I will contact the governor of Alexandria and request that the soldiers be sent. I only hope there is time."

Magbe left and went to his room. He quickly took the flasks and hurried toward the southern sector of the biosphere.

It was in the rain forest biome that he began to unfold his plan. He went to the central water supply, a water supply that was synthetically created within the walls of the biosphere. The rain forest biome was but one of the integral parts of the biosphere's water production system. From the far end the desert biome created heat, which rose and crossed the small ocean biome, collecting moisture. Over the rain forest biome, the moist air, pushed along by a central fan system, turned to rain. The rain then percolated down and was collected in a large reservoir beneath the surface.

This was the water-producing method devised for all biospheres to provide water during the Cataclysm.

He poured the flasks into the water system and left the biome, knowing his followers had been instructed to store water for several days.

Chapter Twelve

Captain Ernst Koehloff was impressed beyond imagination with *Sea Stallion*. It consisted of a weapons platform mounted on a hovercraft designed to move rapidly over water on a cushion of air; the craft could also move across soil, though not with the same speed. Koehloff was from Germany, where he had grown up in the Berlin Biosphere. Now, at thirty-three, the blond, blue-eyed son of a physicist was attached to AfriKorps.

Not since World War II had a Koehloff been to North Africa. None had ever sailed down the Suez Canal, as he was now doing.

The canal was beginning to return to its pre-Cataclysm depth as the poles were once again freezing and the water of the earth began recession.

"Hard to believe there's a city beneath this spot." The voice of Captain Bruce Wills, the *Sea Stallion* captain, spoke over the hum of the hovercraft's solar powered turbine fans.

"Suez," replied Koehloff. "Gateway to the Red Sea." He pointed to the east. "I wonder what Israel looks like?"

Wills shook his head. "There's been no contact established with the Israeli biospheres."

"Inundated?"

"Possible. The Cataclysm caused a great deal of earth movement. Israel was historically susceptible to earthquakes. You do know what happened on the west coast of the United States."

"Yes. The San Andreas Fault separated from the coastal shelf. The Los Angeles Biosphere was swept into the sea. That could be the fate of the Israelis."

"We'll know in a few weeks. A contact team will be entering the coast from the sea." Wills turned the *Sea Stallion* to the west. With the flick of a finger he fired a missile. The missile streaked skyward, then snaked to the west. Wills turned on a television screen. From the nose of the missile a camera began transmitting. Wills studied the screen then pointed. "Cairo."

On the screen a huge biosphere rose from the desert sand. Crumbled buildings lay around the biosphere, rubble that was once a part of a city of millions of inhabitants. The water reached to within five miles of the biosphere.

"My God," Koehloff mumbled.

"The first time you've seen a city that was abandoned before the Cataclysm?"

"No. Berlin looked much the same. It's just difficult to imagine what happened to all those people."

"They died a horrible death. Just like in the United States. Only those who took the pills were spared a hellish death."

Koehloff knew that throughout the world nearly three billion people had been forsaken at the outset of the Cataclysm. It was estimated that roughly one billion took the cyanide capsules offered by the various governments as a humanitarian gesture. Two billion chose to take their chances with nature. It was estimated that only one percent of that population and their offspring survived the Cataclysm.

Koehloff looked up as Major Creighton walked onto the bridge.

"Are your men ready?" asked Wills.

TC nodded. "Ready and raring. They hate being on water."

Wills laughed. "I'd hate being in a tank. Too confining."

TC shrugged. "You get used to it." He glanced at the screen. The picture of the city of Cairo was frozen. "Any contact with the biosphere?"

"I used the frequencies given to me in Alexandria. No response."

"No response? That's odd."

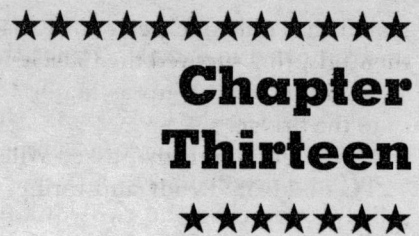

Chapter Thirteen

★★★★★★★

In the forward hull of *Sea Stallion* Silver Allenbey-Creighton carefully opened the rear door of the single medical vehicle assigned to the patrol. She was nauseous from the trip in the confined vehicle. With her was a medical technician named Brooks, a young man of twenty-three fresh from the United States.

"TC's going to have a fit when he sees you."

"Let him. I'm here and it's too late. Come on. I feel the ship slowing. We must be getting ready to debark."

The forward motion of the craft soon settled and the sound of the hum lessened to a soft purr. Inside the vehicle Silver was watching through a periscope as the forward ramp of the *Sea Stallion* opened. The light filled the hull, allowing her to see the four tanks to her immediate front. Ribald's Chariot was the first through the opening; the others followed and then the medical vehicle.

The convoy lumbered onto the sandy beach where she saw Creighton standing with his hands on his hips. He raised one hand, motioning the vehicles to specific positions.

Row after row of four MBTs sat on line while three

IFVs took up the right and left flank of each row.

He turned to Puhaly. "Order the medical vehicle to the rear of the MBTs."

She could see he looked concerned.

"Something's wrong," she whispered to Brooks.

"How do you know?"

"TC's placing the two squadrons of MBTs in frontal assault formation."

She saw Creighton climb into his MBT. Moments later his voice crackled over the radio. "Maintain slow forward speed. There's no response from the biosphere. We're going in easy." His voice ended.

The sky overhead crackled as another recoverable missile streaked toward the blue heaven. Silver knew the missile would provide forward reconnaissance that TC could monitor over his computer inside the MBT.

The missile began reporting in a matter of minutes. In his tank, Creighton could see the biosphere. "Can you give me higher resolution and increased magnification?" Creighton asked Wills.

"On the way." Wills pressed a few buttons on a digital control panel. The photograph of the biosphere intensified.

Creighton's eyes narrowed. "What's that at the main entrance?"

Aboard *Sea Stallion*, Wills studied the intensified photograph. "Let's take a closer look."

"Roger," replied Creighton.

The missile intensified the picture. Then he saw something that warned him off.

"Squadrons . . . halt and hold your position."

Puhaly looked up from the gunner's seat. "What's happening?"

Creighton leaned forward until his nose nearly touched the screen.

More than a dozen bodies lay strewn across the front entrance to the biosphere.

★★★★★★★★★★★★★★
Chapter Fourteen
★★★★★★★

An hour later Creighton's two squadrons continued the vigil in front of the main entrance. Through *Sea Stallion* he had contacted Colonel Clayton. Clayton was emphatic when he ordered, "You are not to enter the biosphere until you know what's going on. Is that understood?"

"Roger." Creighton switched the radio frequency to the internal net. "Reno . . . take eight men and recon the main entrance."

The whir of Falken's IFV droned steadily until the infantry fighting vehicle reached the main entrance. The gate measured thirty feet wide and twenty feet high. The heavy magnetic lock on the massive door was in the OPEN position.

Reno climbed out of the IFV and approached the gate cautiously. Pausing at one of the bodies he could see they were security personnel by their uniforms. He knelt and examined the bodies. Their lips were swollen, eyes bulged nearly out of the sockets, and a red rash covered all exposed skin. Falken grabbed the communicator on his harness.

"Something strange, TC."

"Describe the bodies."

While Falken was describing the bodies, Silver

Allenbey-Creighton was on the bridge of the *Sea Stallion*. She listened carefully to Reno's detailed account.

"Can you see anything inside the entrance?" asked Creighton.

"No. I'll recon the entrance now."

Creighton couldn't have been more surprised as he heard a familiar—but unexpected—voice, blare over the radio.

"No! Don't go in there, Reno!"

Creighton jerked upright. "What in hell are you doing here!" he demanded.

"This is no time for a domestic spat, TC. This is serious. Dead serious. I came here because this same type of virus infected a family in Alexandria. They had come to Alexandria from Cairo. You must not go inside without protection."

Creighton's teeth clamped shut. "God dammit." He thought for a moment. "Reno . . . take four men and climb into your SIPE suits. Don't enter the biosphere until you're fully protected from biological agents. Is that clear?"

"Clear." Reno pointed at four of his men. "Let's get it on."

They went to the rear of the IFV. From a storage locker they removed five SIPE suits—Soldier Integrated Protective Equipment—suits that would make them self-contained in the face of any chemical or biological contamination. The suits sealed completely, and were air-conditioned to allow comfort in any type of weather; a helmet with integrated sighting and heads-up display, capable of utilizing thermal imaging, gave the soldiers their battle-sighting capability. The suit was made of bullet-proof material, and once it was on, the soldier was virtually impervious to outside influences.

"Ready to rock 'n' roll," Reno reported.

"Move out." Creighton watched the men through his binoculars. When they disappeared through the entrance, he heard Silver say, "Tell them not to touch anything with their bare hands."

"They know that. They're not idiots. Not like some people I know."

Before he could say anything else he heard the distinctive report of automatic weapons fire.

★★★★★★★★★★★★★
Chapter Fifteen
★★★★★★★

What Reno Falken found waiting for him inside the biosphere was more than he expected. Beyond the entrance, inside the structure, was an open area much like a parade ground. That was where Falken first saw the human carnage. Bodies littered the entire area; hundreds of bodies. A flock of vultures had somehow found their way through the entrance and were ravaging the corpses.

Falken fired another burst, killing a vulture that was tearing the flesh from the body of a young man.

"Jesus, TC. There must be hundreds of dead bodies." His eyes swept upward, to the upper levels. He saw no movement.

"What the hell was the shooting?"

"Buzzards. The place is filled with them. There must be thousands."

The black shapes of the vultures loomed from everywhere, specking the inside with their ominous forms.

Silver's voice interrupted. "Close the doors. The vultures must not be allowed to leave. The virus could spread beyond the Biosphere."

Creighton heard more gunfire. Falken's men were systematically killing all of the vultures. The air filled with the flapping of wings as hundreds of buzzards raced through the open door. Finally the door was closed, but there were still hundreds left inside.

"Let's get to it," Falken whispered.

The gunfire mixed with the roar of the flapping wings, turning the interior of the biosphere into a din of horror. Falken knelt and coolly fired systematically, locating his targets through the thermal imaging of the weapons targeting system. He didn't have to move the weapon, which was mounted on a pommel at his waist. He only had to locate the target and press a button on his wrist mounted firing pod.

The black creatures began falling from overhead, where most had sought refuge. There was none. With systematic calm, Falken and his men sighted, locked up each target, and fired. Hundreds lay dead on the parade field, wings fluttering in the final throes of death. Some of the vultures, guided by instinct, and though wounded, tried to consume their fallen brethren.

"Christ," whispered Falken.

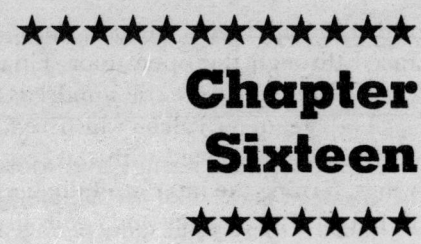

Chapter Sixteen

Thirty minutes later the last of the vultures had been dispatched. Falken sent two men up to the first level; he took the other two to the second level.

They began an area search of each level, carefully searching, discovering more death with each step.

Reaching a large room, Falken figured this was the main meeting hall. Most biospheres had been designed similarly, and what he expected to find behind the doors took him by surprise.

"Praise Allah, you have come." Magbe was rushing toward Falken. He had a rag to his nose.

In the room were nearly two hundred other inhabitants of the biosphere. Falken flipped a switch on his communication system, allowing his voice to project externally.

"What has happened here?"

Magbe's eyes widened. "We do not know. People started dying yesterday. Hundreds. Maybe more than a thousand."

"What was the cause?"

Magbe shrugged.

Silver's voice echoed in Falken's ear. "You need to draw a blood sample, Reno. I need one sample."

Reno looked at Magbe. "Where's the hospital?"

Magbe led Falken to the biosphere hospital. The beds and floors were littered with dead bodies. A surgeon lay across the chest of a dead woman on an operating table.

Falken found a syringe and took a blood sample from a dead body. "Got the sample," he reported.

"You say there's still some people alive?" she asked.

"Affirmative. Approximately two hundred."

"Take a sample from one of the survivors."

Falken looked at Magbe. "I need a sample of your blood."

Magbe rolled up his sleeve and extended his arm.

Falken drew the blood, then sent the two samples back to Creighton with one of his men.

Magbe introduced himself. "I am grateful you have come. You heard our pleas."

Falken shook his head. "We knew nothing of this. We were sent here on other matters."

"What matters?"

Falken didn't answer, he merely said, "You'll have to get that information from Major Creighton."

"As you wish."

Falken felt his skin crawl. "Any idea what happened here?"

Magbe's mouth tightened. He said, "I have no idea. People became suddenly ill."

"Did they suffer long?'

He shook his head. "Once the symptoms began, death followed quickly. We did not know what to do. The medical personnel died before they could be of assistance."

"You know, the biosphere may have to be destroyed."

Magbe nodded. "We discussed that last night. We

were going to destroy the biosphere to prevent contamination from reaching the outside."

Falken grumped. "You might have begun by closing the main entrance. Vultures have been inside. The contamination may have spread to the outside."

"We did not think."

"Why didn't you contact Alexandria?"

"The communications personnel went insane. They destroyed the equipment. The antennas. We had no way of contacting the outside."

"What about food and water?"

"We are afraid to eat or drink anything."

"Good idea. We have supplies. Get your people organized and bring them to the parade field. We need to start gathering the bodies. Men and women will have to be formed into burial details."

Magbe nodded and walked away. When he reached the meeting hall his followers stood in silence as he went to the podium. "They are convinced," he whispered.

The excitement threading through the followers of the Hakama was barely suppressed.

"What do we do now?" asked Abu.

"Nothing," came the reply from a man sitting in the rear of the hall. All eyes turned to the man who was wearing a *khaffeyeh* to cover his features. Where the cloth was wrapped around his face, his eyes burned fiercely.

The man walked to Magbe and stood at his side. "Soon . . . we will have all the equipment we need," said Benhaddou.

PART TWO: THE NOSTRADAMUS PROJECT

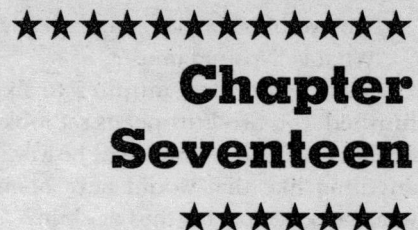

Chapter Seventeen

"Damn!" Colonel Clayton couldn't believe what he was hearing. He left the communications center at Base Camp One and returned to his office. In minutes he had contacted the commanders of the multinational force. Thirty minutes later they met in his office.

"We could be dealing with widespread disease of the sort unseen since before the Cataclysm," Colonel Marie Forchette of the French army, noted as she listened to Clayton's summation of the situation in Cairo.

Colonel Dieter Preuss of the German contingency concurred. "The question is, what are we going to do to contain the disease in that area?"

Clayton offered up what they all knew. "There are still thousands of nomads roaming that part of the desert. Each one is a potential carrier."

"That could be catastrophic," said Forchette.

"There is an option. One that would ensure the disease does not spread out of a certain geographical area."

Nothing was said. They didn't know what he meant.

"What other option?" asked Forchette.

Clayton spoke a single word: "Nostradamus."

The two officers looked quizzically at Clayton.

"What is 'Nostradamus'?"

Clayton took ten minutes to explain. When he finished, the two Europeans sat looking aghast.

"My God." Preuss breathed heavily. "I never thought anything like that would have been developed after what happened prior to the Cataclysm."

"Don't be naïve, Preuss," snapped Clayton. "We would have used it on the Marauders were it not for all the nomads that would have been affected. What kept the weapon in the pouch was the fact so many thousands of innocent people would have been killed unnecessarily. In this case, we're looking at different circumstances. Nothing is sacred. Not even our own personnel."

"Who else knows about this weapon, Colonel?" asked Forchette.

"A few Americans, and the Central Committee."

Preuss shook his head. "This decision must be made by the Central Committee of the United Nations. Not by one person."

Clayton agreed. The recently re-formed United Nations was composed of member nations able to participate in international government following the Cataclysm. The decision to initiate Nostradamus would have to be decided by heads of state.

"I'll contact President Dawson. He'll determine if the weapon is to be involved in this matter."

"Is there any other option?" asked Forchette. "The disease can't be transmitted through airborne contact. Nor through touch. Only by direct transmission, such as ingestion. Food. Water. Isn't there another way?"

Clayton thought for a moment. "I don't know. You tell me . . . how do you contain the flight of buzzards? You know as well as I that those damn vultures are a major food source of desert nomads. Hell, even in the United States the hostiles would take their dead and use them as bait to trap vultures. If it weren't for reptiles and vultures half the hostiles wouldn't have survived the Cataclysm in DesFor. Now we're faced with the spreading of a disease that could be catastrophic to the regions outside the immediate area."

Forchette nodded her agreement. "If that's our decision then we better get started."

"Yes. We have to get started. Something like this doesn't happen with the snap of a finger. The scientists who developed Nostradamus are in the United States. The launch facility is in the United States. If the Central Committee approves, it'll take time to get the weapon in place."

Preuss lifted a finger. "One question, Colonel: what is the size of the region that will be affected?"

Clayton shrugged his shoulders. "How large an area do you think we should consider, Colonel?"

Preuss thought for a moment. "I would start small, say, one hundred miles."

"One hundred miles. What if that's not a large enough area?" asked Forchette.

The German looked at Clayton slyly. "In that case I would suggest the United States could use a similar weapon. There are more, aren't there, Colonel?'

Clayton didn't answer; he went to a map of North Africa. He carefully studied the area that would be affected. He placed his thumb on Cairo and rotated his hand in a circle. He marked four cardinal points of the compass. "This is the area we should consider initially. Once that area has been decontaminated we can do a follow-up investigation. If the spread is contained . . . we're out of the woods. If not, we can expand the area."

Preuss smiled lightly. His question had been answered.

Chapter Eighteen

Biosphere One. United States.

Biosphere One rose from the night like a great monolith; a solitary structure measuring 400 feet in height, 6,000 meters on each of the four sides. Enclosed by thick, durable polymer glass, the structure was resilient, composed of low-weight, high-strength, heat-resistant titanium beams and girders.

As a child, Woolford Dawson, the president of the United States—like all the ancestors of the current population of "specials"—called the structure Uranus. Somewhere in the past one of the specials learned in their Greek mythology class that Uranus had been called the Father of Titans.

The name stuck—unofficially, of course.

The capital of the United States was still officially known as Biosphere One. It had once been called Washington, D.C., but that was before the great Cataclysm.

President Dawson was sleeping deeply when he was awakened by the buzzing of his bedside telephone. He rose slowly, his muscles, now aging, feeling more and more the effects of injuries suffered in his youth.

He knew immediately the call was coming over GROUNDSTAR, the surface telecommunications linkup now established throughout the world to allow governments to converse on matters of mutual interest. Unlike satellite communications of the twenty-first century, now nonexistent, GROUNDSTAR gave off a revealing buzz.

He said hello, then began listening. The voice of Colonel Thomas Clayton was familiar. He had known Dawson for many years, and was the president's first choice to lead the American contingent destined to help form the central element of AfriKorps. They were friends and could speak openly.

"Give me your estimation of a worse-case scenario," the president said.

"Vultures are territorial so long as there is a food source. Once that dies out they move to other areas. We know that vultures are still used as a human food source in some areas. According to Major Creighton's report the disease is transferable through tissue consumption and water consumption. Wherever the vultures become a food source or find water there is the potential for spreading the disease."

"Can the disease be spread through airborne contact?"

"The physician with Major Creighton's patrol said the disease can be spread only orally. Either through food, or water. Otherwise, there would have been no survivors in Cairo."

Dawson thought about something that bothered him. "I find it curious there were so many survivors. Why was that?"

There was a pause. "The report states that the survivors were sleeping. They woke up to absolute chaos. It was apparent from the outset that the water source had been affected. Precautions were taken at that point."

"What is being done with the survivors?"

"The survivors are remaining in Cairo . . . unless the Nostradamus option is exercised."

"Thomas, what is your suggestion? I mean, from your gut? Do you think the situation is that critical? Damn. I hate to exercise Nostradamus . . . we're not quite sure of its far-reaching effects."

This time Clayton paused. "I suggest we put the weapon system in place. At the same time we send out patrols and determine the scope of the contamination. But I strongly suggest we have the weapon in place in case it's needed."

Dawson thought this a realistic request. "I'll have to have approval of the Committee before I can give the go-ahead to launch."

"I'm aware of that, sir."

"Which means I'll need some hard facts. First, how many people will be directly affected by the application?"

"I have rough figures that indicate approximately 8,000 nomads. Of course, the Alexandria and Cairo biospheres will have to be evacuated out of harm's way."

"What about evacuating the nomads?"

Clayton automatically shook his head. "There won't be enough time, Mr. President. Contamination may already have begun."

"What about inoculation?"

"Again, time is the factor. Major Creighton's physician has a limited supply of the serum. The technology is not at her disposal to develop enough serum to inoculate thousands of people, if we're even able to locate that many. I'm afraid it's damned if we do and damned if we don't."

"What about our alien friends? Can they be of help?" Dawson knew that the technology of the alien spacecraft, built to resemble an American city of the twenty-first century, was sitting on the outskirts of Clayton's base in North Africa.

"Disease is their greatest fear, Mr. President. They can re-create life . . . but they can't help those already affected."

"Why?"

"They must have a blood sample prior to death. We don't have blood samples from the nomads. Any blood sample we took would contain the virus. Either way . . . the nomads are dead."

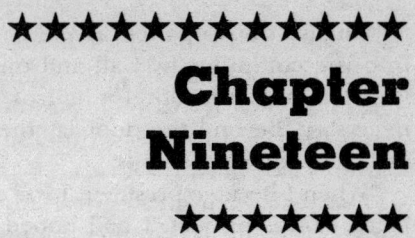

Chapter Nineteen

Biosphere One. United States.
0800.

Ten miles from Biosphere One, Dr. Phillip Call was sitting at his desk when he heard the buzzer ring from the outer gate. He switched on a television monitor and watched the guard at the front gate approach a vehicle bearing the flag of the president. He smoothed back his hair and rose from his desk, then walked hurriedly toward the door. He took the elevator to the first level and arrived as the president was escorted into the facility code-named Black Chamber.

President Dawson looked around curiously. "This is my first visit to your facility, Dr. Call."

The two men shook hands, then the doctor escorted the president to an elevator. The two rode the elevator eight stories beneath the surface. When the door opened they were confronted by several armed guards.

"Your palm print, Mr. President." Call motioned toward a palm identification unit.

The president pressed both palms onto the identifier. Seconds later a green light glowed.

Dr. Call did the same and saw the green light. Both were cleared for entry into the vault.

A heavy door opened as the code was punched into the computer by Call and one of the guards. Neither knew the other's half of the code. It was necessary. Beyond the door lay the weapons system code-named Nostradamus.

"When I became president I was quite surprised to learn of this project. I had hoped we would never again see such weapons of destruction manufactured on earth."

"It was a hedge against the future, Mr. President. Our ancestors weren't certain what we would find beyond the walls of our biospheres once the Cataclysm ended."

"What we found was a living hell."

"Certainly. But it wasn't a hell that wasn't extinguishable. Twenty years before cessation there wasn't that assurance."

"This project took twenty years to develop?"

Call merely smiled and motioned with a sweep of his arm.

Dawson felt a chill run up his spine. Inside the vault, he was standing on a catwalk that overlooked a deep cavern carved into the earth and reinforced by heavy steel girders. At the center of the cavern were a dozen circular steel covers enclosing deep silos.

"How long will it take you to get one of these devices operational?" asked the president.

Call thought for a moment. "Twenty-four hours for launch preparation."

"What is the range?"

"Twelve thousand miles."

"And the diameter of destruction?"

Call answered quickly, "One hundred miles in diameter."

"Can you break that down for me?"

Call thought for a moment, then began drawing a series of circles in the empty air. The first circle was very small. "The immediate blast area will extend twenty-five miles."

He drew another circle in the air. This circle seemed larger, consuming the first circle. "The second area of effect will extend another twenty-five miles. That will consist of the firestorm, limited in comparison to the range of a nuclear weapon. What the blast doesn't consume, the firestorm will incinerate."

"I was informed the diameter required would be approximately one hundred miles."

"Correct." He drew another circle outside the imaginary blast and fireball circles. "The final zone will extend another fifty miles. Since we are talking a desert environment, each particle of sand at that point will literally become a projectile, traveling at a velocity somewhere near eight hundred feet per second."

"Good God."

"As you can see . . . the bomb is quite effective in this environment. Of course, radiation will claim anything within the three zones that might survive."

"In other words: no form of living organism can survive the effects?"

Call shook his head. "Not a living soul. Not man . . . nor animal, nor microorganisms in the air or water. The entire area will be void of life. The life of the radiation is minimal. And, it is an isolated part of the world. Not much to be lost."

Dawson ignored that comment for fear he might strangle the bastard. "When did you say this type of weapon was developed?"

"In the twentieth century. But it was never deployed."

The president looked sad, "My God, Dr. Call . . . I may become the first president in American history to approve the launch of a neutron intercontinental ballistic missile!"

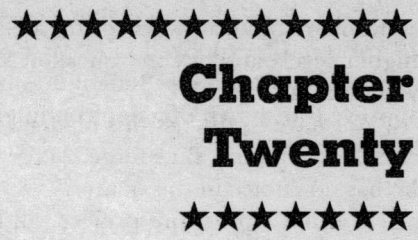

Chapter Twenty

★★★★★★★★

"Jesus, Joseph, and Mary!" Roman Standish invoked the hierarchy of the spiritual world, yet he knew that mankind had again been left to its own devices. The message that arrived from Clayton had torn him from a deep sleep, the first he had known in weeks since his arrival in Alexandria. What he despised most was the quick and seemingly heartless manner Clayton had used to inform him of the events unfolding. Especially where the Nostradamus Project was concerned.

"You can't be serious!" Roman had muttered as he fought through the sleepy haze.

"It's our only option," the commander of AfriKorps had replied. Minutes before he had received word from President Dawson of the Committee's reluctant approval of the use of the weapon to cauterize the desert area believed to be infected.

"Thousands of lives will be lost, Thomas."

"Those lives would have been lost regardless. Hundreds of thousands may be saved," was the curt reply.

Roman knew Clayton had not opted for the weapon without weighing all the ramifications, including the moral responsibility of such a decision.

Roman could only accept the decision of those at higher levels and ask the question simply, "What do you want me to do?"

"You have to discuss this matter with the governor of the Alexandria Biosphere. Make him understand he has no choice in this matter."

"In other words, the project will be implemented regardless of his cooperation?"

"Precisely. There is too much at stake."

"How long do we have?"

"Twenty-four hours. Colt Derider is there with his roadbed contraption and the Iron Horse. You will load the people onto the train and debark immediately."

"What about the people in Cairo?"

"Major Creighton will receive the same orders. He is to evacuate the biosphere and take the survivors overland to your location."

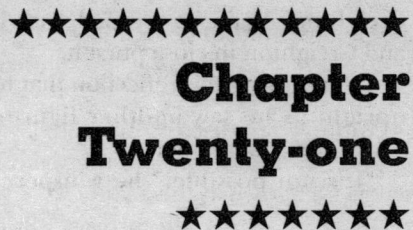

Chapter Twenty-one

Benhaddou watched his enemy through binoculars as Creighton stood before the survivors of the murderous scheme. His anger was barely contained as he heard Creighton's words echo through the structure over the PA system.

"We will leave in one hour. Take nothing except the clothes on your back. Food will be provided en route by our troops."

"We will never survive the desert," a man shouted.

"You won't survive here. It's your choice. Either prepare to move out . . . or you'll be left behind."

Eyes suddenly fell on Magbe. The leader of what they thought was the new order, guided by their fidelity to Allah, said nothing. He turned and looked upward, toward the room where Benhaddou was hiding.

Benhaddou slowly scanned the crowd. The soldiers of AfriKorps were standing behind Creighton. He recalled Creighton, and how the soldier had destroyed his army; had chased him through the desert and captured him. Had him tried and imprisoned. He had escaped from the prison, killing several guards and making his way south toward the Marauder lines, only to be confronted once again by

Creighton. Again he escaped, with his brother Shona and Creighton in close pursuit.

It was during this reflection that he suddenly bolted upright as he saw another figure appear near the AfriKorps commander.

"It's not possible!" he whispered. Yet, there she was.

Creighton's woman!

"I killed her. I tore her eyes out in the desert! This is not possible."

He could only stare at the woman in amazement.

Captain Silver Allenbey-Creighton was wearing an armband with the red cross emblazoned.

Benhaddou had not anticipated this turn of events: the evacuation of the biosphere before he and the followers of Magbe could overpower the soldiers and steal their weaponry. He had not considered that he would see the living representation of a woman he had murdered nearly two years before.

It was then an idea began to formulate. He raised the binoculars again and studied the woman.

A leer crossed his lips. He knew how he could still have what he wanted . . . and settle an old score.

First he needed sleep. He crawled into Magbe's bed, falling asleep to visions of what he would do to Creighton's woman.

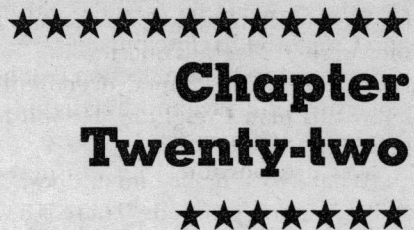

Chapter Twenty-two

0800.

The following morning, the survivors of the biosphere moved slowly from their quarters toward the assembly area beyond the huge doors of the biosphere. The troops of AfriKorps had assembled dozens of transports from the biosphere motor pool and were beginning to load the people.

Puhaly took command of the loading. Silver was moving hurriedly through the group, watching for those who might show signs of sickness. She found none.

Creighton had contacted Clayton with the message that the convoy would depart within the hour. *Sea Stallion* had been dispatched back to the river with orders to move north to the sea.

High above the floor of the parade field a small group of conspirators gathered to make a final decision.

"All is lost!" moaned Semir. He was staring at Magbe with the pained look of a kicked dog.

"Silence!" snapped Benhaddou. "You sound like children."

"Then what do you suggest? If we refuse to leave, the AfriKorps will become suspicious," said Magbe.

He was with Benhaddou, Amina, and his four followers; they were in Magbe's quarters.

An evil look swarmed over Benhaddou's face. "I know this man Creighton. He will follow orders, but he will also disobey orders."

"What would make him disobey?" asked Magbe.

Benhaddou grinned. "There is a way!"

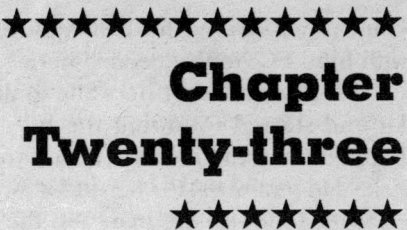

Chapter Twenty-three

1200.

"It is now imperative that you evacuate the remaining personnel to the Alexandria Biosphere. Photo reconnaissance has confirmed the deaths of hundreds of nomads from the contamination."

"I'm trying, Colonel. Dammit, these people are moving slower than cold honey. I've sent a detail into the biosphere to make a final check for anyone that might have been left behind."

Creighton was furious when Puhaly approached with more bad news. "TC, these damned gas-guzzling vehicles of theirs won't last the trip. We're going to be moving at a waltz at best."

"Then turn up the music, Steve. We don't have anything else to use. They sure as hell can't walk!"

Before Puhaly could say anything else, a young boy ran to him.

"Please, major, my mother. She has become ill."

Creighton cursed. "I've got to sign off, Colonel. We've got a problem. I'll check back with you when we're ready for departure. Out." He turned to the boy. "Where is your mother?"

The boy pointed toward the biosphere. Before he

could say anything he heard Silver's voice. "I'll go with him, TC. You're needed here."

The boy smiled at her. She grabbed her medical kit and started following the boy. A man suddenly stepped from the crowd. "Thank you. My wife is very sick." He motioned for her to follow.

Silver followed the man and the boy into the biosphere. They went to the main elevator, where she watched the man press the button for the top floor. The ride was swift, and when the door opened, she started to step forward. Then she gasped.

"God! No!" Then she saw only blackness as the hard fist of Benhaddou struck her jaw.

Benhaddou looked at the boy. "Go now. Tell the soldiers!"

He stepped back into the elevator, not noticing the bodies of four AfriKorps soldiers lying strewn along the corridor the tall black man was now traveling with the woman over his shoulder.

Benhaddou, followed by Magbe and the others, raced toward an elevator at the far end of the corridor. The door closed.

"This is a maintenance elevator. We will come out in the rear of the biosphere," said Magbe. He looked at Benhaddou. "Where are your tanks?"

Benhaddou pointed to the west. "One kilometer from here. They are buried beneath the sand. We can be there before Creighton figures out we've left the biosphere."

"Then what?" asked Magbe.

Again Benhaddou laughed. "He will follow!"

★★★★★★★★★★★★★
Chapter Twenty-four
★★★★★★★

It was thirty minutes later that Creighton discovered Silver's absence, and that was by mere chance. He had the column loaded and prepared to move out when he was checking the rear vehicles. That's where he found Brooks walking nervously back and forth in the sand.

Suddenly the boy appeared. He told Creighton what had happened. Within seconds he had a patrol reenter the biosphere. That's where the grisly discovery of the dead soldiers set off the second warning that something was wrong.

It was in the main security center that Creighton discovered the treachery of an old enemy. Abe was standing at a television monitor, watching the replay of one of the biosphere's security cameras. The tape was frozen, with the face of Benhaddou framed clearly.

"Impossible!" Creighton breathed. He ran the tape back several seconds, then watched again as the murder of his men was cruelly reenacted. Then he saw the part where Silver was taken. His eyes followed the image of Benhaddou until he disappeared into the elevator.

Reaching his MBT, Creighton hurriedly called Colonel Clayton. The reaction was not to his liking.

"I'm sorry, Abe. But you have your orders. You are to proceed directly to Alexandria ASAP. The train is waiting. You must get those people and your personnel out of the blast area. We've run out of time."

"Delay the blast. I only need a few hours, goddammit. She's my wife. I won't leave her!"

There was a momentary delay, then, "You have your orders. I'm sorry." The GROUNDSTAR link was disconnected.

Creighton slammed the microphone against the console in his MBT. He stared hatefully toward the desert. Puhaly was sitting in his gunner's seat inside the tank, looking up at Creighton.

"Fuck the orders, TC. Let's go get her back."

Creighton thought for a moment, then called Falken. Reno Falken was there in a matter of seconds. Creighton detailed the plan he had quickly devised.

"Armbrust and Falken will take the convoy to Alexandria. I'm taking my MBT and following them."

Armbrust said what they all had avoided. "She may already be dead."

Creighton shook his head. "No. He wouldn't have burdened himself with a hostage if he intended to kill her. He wants something more."

"He wants you to follow," Puhaly said acidly.

"Right. And that's what he's going to get." He looked at the gunner, and Fergus Felot, the driver of Ribald's Chariot. "Are you in this with me?'

There was no hesitation of either man. "We're in," both said simultaneously.

Creighton took the microphone and contacted Bruce Wills aboard *Sea Stallion*. Wills agreed to fire a missile with the television scan. Creighton watched impatiently as the television screen eventually began beaming a picture from a missile fired aboard the hovercraft. The Cairo Biosphere came into view; as did the convoy of vehicles staged in front of the biosphere. Gradually the camera began depicting the rear of the biosphere.

Creighton zoomed in on the trail left in the sand at the rear. The trail ended less than a kilometer away. In the sand, Creighton saw what appeared to be two large holes.

"Tanks," Creighton said softly. "The bastard had two of our MBTs buried in the sand. No wonder we didn't see anything."

"Who was looking?" asked Puhaly.

Creighton's index finger tapped the signature etched into the sand by the tanks. "The tracks are leading south. Toward the Pyramids of Saqqâra."

Chapter Twenty-five

Silver woke up with thunder crashing in her head. Her first thoughts were that somehow she had been saved from Benhaddou since she was riding in an MBT. She recognized the interior; the tank was identical to TC's MBT. Then she saw through the veil of darkness the outline of Benhaddou's head, and she knew she was far from being safe.

She said nothing. She just listened to the discussion between Magbe and Benhaddou. "Your followers know what they're supposed to do?" asked Benhaddou.

"They know. Just before the convoy begins the march through the desert they will overpower the soldiers."

"Good. You were right. It would have been more difficult to try to destroy the soldiers in the biosphere. Once they're in the desert the forces will be more spread out. Capture of the vehicles intact is important."

"Nothing will happen to the equipment. We will use the soldiers as hostages to guarantee we are not interfered with. What about the woman? Why did you want her?"

Benhaddou laughed. "Her husband is the AfriKorps officer . . . Major Creighton. I want to separate him from his men. He is quite formidable. He might have discovered what you were planning. This way he will follow his woman."

"Are you certain?"

"I am certain. That's why I have not killed her."

Then Silver's voice broke into the conversation. "You've done nothing except trick yourself, Benhaddou."

The Morocc looked down to where Silver sat strapped into the auxiliary jumpseat behind the gunner's chair. "What do you mean?"

"In a few hours this entire part of the country is going to be destroyed."

"Why?" asked Magbe.

"You fool. The disease that killed your people. It must not be allowed to spread. The vultures will carry the contamination to other areas. My government has ordered the total destruction of this area."

"How?" snapped Benhaddou.

Silver looked directly at Magbe. "In a few hours a missile will carry a bomb that will destroy all forms of life for one hundred miles in diameter. That's why we were taking your people to Alexandria. To get them out of harm's way. Now you're leading them to their death."

"She lies. There is no such weapon." said Benhaddou.

"There is. It's called a neutron bomb. It can destroy all forms of life. You don't have a chance if you stay in the desert."

Magbe turned to Benhaddou. "What do we do?"

Benhaddou looked at Silver. "She is lying. There's

no such weapon. We continue with our plan. But first ... I will kill Creighton."

Silver felt a wave of nausea thread through her body. She had to warn TC. But how?

Chapter Twenty-six

★★★★★★★★

"I don't like it," said Puhaly. He was studying the set of tank tracks through his battlesight, noting the direction was due south.

"For once I happen to agree with Steve," added Fergus. The driver was watching through a periscope, and he felt as though he was being led into a trap.

"You're right," Creighton said sharply.

"Then what in hell are we doing?" asked Puhaly.

Creighton had felt uneasy about the turn of events since arriving at the biosphere. It was as though another force was guiding their movements. "I haven't trusted that bastard Magbe since we met him. I have a feeling there's others as well."

Puhaly bolted upright in his seat. "The convoy?"

Creighton nodded as his eyes remained glued to the tank tracks. "I'd say that's Benhaddou's plan. Why else would he show up in this part of the world? The Riersgard patrol was hundreds of miles to the west. There's no reason for him to come in this direction unless he was brought here."

"One of Magbe's people?" asked Felot.

Creighton took the microphone. "Creighton to Falken."

Reno Falken's voice came over the radio. He was

trailing behind the MBT in an infantry fighting vehicle. "Reno . . . get back to the convoy. I have an idea we're being had." Creighton switched to another frequency. "Captain Armbrust . . . what's the situation?"

Armbrust's voice came over the radio. From the tone of his voice there appeared nothing wrong. "Situation is stable. We're moving north at a speed the transports can handle. Slow, but sure."

"Notice anything unusual?"

"Negative. But there is a message for you from Colonel Clayton."

"What's the message?" He knew he was about to hear a blistering reproach for his action.

"The colonel said 'good luck and good hunting.'"

Creighton reached and switched off the radio. Puhaly looked up at Creighton. There was a tightness around the gunner's eyes as he spoke. "'Good luck and good hunting'? That's bullshit."

Creighton nodded. "Something's wrong."

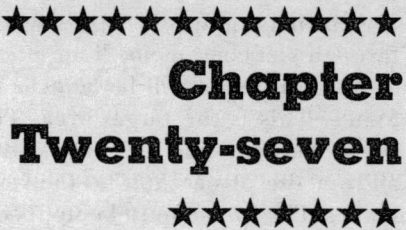

Chapter Twenty-seven

★★★★★★★★

Abu lowered the pistol from Armbrust's head. He leered at the soldier, then he adjusted the frequency on the radio. He took the microphone from the captured AfriKorps soldier and said proudly, "Abu to Magbe. We have captured the column!"

Armbrust and his men had been totally surprised. The overpowering of his men came so swiftly—so unexpectedly—he thought it was a joke at first. Then he saw that Abu's men all held pistols on his men and the nightmare was in full swing.

The AfriKorps soldiers were stripped of their weapons and herded into an area between the biosphere and the vehicles. Armbrust was led away with the other officers. They were taken inside the biosphere, where Abu waited with the others for the return of Magbe and Benhaddou.

Armbrust walked away from the officers and approached Abu. He ran his fingers through his close-cropped hair, then said, "You've made a fatal mistake. You don't know what's going on."

Abu shrugged. "What do you mean?"

Armbrust explained about the neutron bomb.

"You lie!" Abu shouted. He struck at Armbrust's face, but the martial arts expert blocked his hand.

Armbrust gripped Abu's wrist tightly, saying through clenched teeth, "I am not lying. In a matter of hours a missile will be launched from the United States. This is the target area. The leaders of the world are not going to let this contamination spread all over the planet. You let the vultures feed on the bodies. The spread must be stopped."

Abu hurried to Armbrust's MBT. He quickly called Magbe.

In the MBT leading Creighton away from the biosphere, Magbe listened to the message from Abu. He looked at Benhaddou. "What the woman said must be true. The officer could not have made this up. There was no way."

Benhaddou ordered the driver to halt. "Turn around. We go back."

The two tanks swung around, following their tracks. Ten minutes later Benhaddou saw what he expected to find: Major Abe Creighton's tank and the IFV.

Benhaddou ordered the tanks to a halt. He climbed out of the cupola and reached inside. He gripped Silver by the arm and jerked her through the opening. Pushing her into the sand, he took a pistol and aimed at her head. That was when he saw Creighton's tank come to a halt not twenty feet from where he stood.

The tank sat there momentarily; finally, the cupola opened and Creighton climbed onto the hull. Creighton stood silent, then dropped to the sand. He approached Benhaddou cautiously. In the tank, Fergus had a 7.76-caliber coaxial machine gun trained on Benhaddou.

Benhaddou stood with an air of superiority. He

watched Creighton approach until they stood staring into each other's eyes.

Creighton looked at his wife. "Are you all right?"

She nodded. He looked at Benhaddou and said, "This is between you and me. Leave her out of this."

Benhaddou bowed slightly. He motioned at Silver. She stood and stepped to Creighton's side. "He knows about the neutron bomb."

"I figured as much." He looked at Benhaddou. "What now?"

That was when Creighton was taken by total surprise. Benhaddou extended his hand, with the butt of the weapon facing away. "I am your prisoner."

★★★★★★★★★★★★★

PART THREE: ESCAPE

★★★★★★★

Chapter Twenty-eight

"*That sonofabitch is* up to something." Creighton seethed. He was watching Silver as she examined the AfriKorps soldiers. It was late in the afternoon. Time was running against them.

Captain Mike Armbrust was beside Creighton. He was still incensed with the way he had been fooled. "No harm done. But I agree. He's not the sort to throw in the towel so easily."

Puhaly offered a suggestion. "Maybe he saw the futility of the situation. He might have figured it was better to live in prison than to die in the desert."

Creighton was totally unconvinced of this possibility. "Not likely. Which means we watch this bastard like a hawk. Steve, put four men on him, around-the-clock surveillance. And that includes that Magbe character and his friend, Abu. I want them in the same IFV, but treated with equal security. I agree with Mike . . . there's more to come."

Armbrust brought them to the present. "Which means we have to get moving. The time schedule has been delayed enough. We're only going to have enough time to reach Alexandria and load aboard the train."

"Why take them?" Puhaly asked, jerking his thumb at the followers of Magbe. "They would have slit our throats and left us for the buzzards. Let's just leave them. Give them a taste of hellfire from that neutron bomb."

Creighton chuckled. "Because, we're civilized. Let's saddle up. There's a long trip to make and not much time. I'll contact Clayton." He looked at Armbrust. "That was a good signal."

"You should check in with the old man. He's hotter than hell itself."

Creighton went to his MBT and tuned in the frequency of the AfriKorps commander. When Clayton's voice came over the radio, the air shook with his anger.

Finally the CO settled down, and if there was any relief for Abe, it was the fact that Clayton was grateful that Benhaddou had been captured.

"I'll have Shona here to meet your column. He'll be delighted. Now get moving. We're running out of time. The launch is scheduled for twenty-four hundred hours tonight."

"What about the train?"

"It's already shuttling personnel back and forth to the west, outside of the blast zone."

Creighton explained the situation involving the followers of Magbe. "I suggest you watch yourself on your end. I doubt he's operating alone. I'm certain there's more of his people in Alexandria."

"I'll look after things on this end. You get your ass moving. There's no way I can stop this thing from happening. We're running out of time. Reports have come in from patrols in the western sector that contaminated vultures have been discovered, along with indiginous personnel. The spread has already begun."

Creighton went back to where Armbrust and Puhaly waited with Silver. The race across the desert began within minutes.

★★★★★★★★★★★★★
Chapter Twenty-nine
★★★★★★★★

Roman Standish had walked into the desert with a sense of foreboding; what he was going to convey to his friend, he knew, could be met with mixed emotion. And possibly, an uncertain reaction.

He found Shona sitting atop an outcropping of rocks; the tall, black-skinned desert nomad appeared regal against the wash of fading red sunlight. He carried a spear, a long pole with a sharp bayonet attached to one end; a round, hard ball was carved into the other end. The weapon could be used for stabbing, or splitting a skull, a use Roman had seen the nomad employ on several occasions. Unlike the soldiers of AfriKorps, he didn't carry any modern weapon; his was ancient, much like the look in his eyes when Roman approached.

Roman, the philosopher, went directly to the heart of the matter. "Major Creighton has captured your brother."

Shona showed no sign of emotion. His shoulders rose slightly, then settled; his gaze remained on the sun, settling now toward the western horizon.

Finally he spoke, his voice deep, resonant. "I have

felt his presence for several days. Now, I understand."

"He will return to prison. Colonel Clayton is building a special—how do I say this—a cage. A cage aboard the train for his transport."

"It will not hold him." Shona's words were straightforward.

"It will hold him."

Shona shook his head. "He must be killed."

"We do not murder, Shona."

"It is not murder to kill an animal that invades your village and destroys your children."

"Despite what you and Major Creighton feel . . . he is a human being. He must be treated humanely."

"Did he treat his victims with humanity?"

Roman could not respond positively to this question. He knew the answer. The truth. "It is not important for him. It is important for us. To know that we as people do not stoop to his level. To execute is barbaric. It is time for the barbarism to end."

Shona rose and stepped down from the rocks. Never had Roman seen such a look of despair on the face of his friend. Never had he seen such a look of pain. "I must go," was all he said.

Shona walked away, toward the south. Roman knew in his heart that his friend was not walking into the desert to seek solitude. Rather, he was walking toward the moment both men knew would one day come.

The moment brother met brother in the heat of battle.

Roman stood quietly watching. When the figure of the nomad disappeared against the horizon, he lifted the skirt of his toga and hurried toward the Alexandria Biosphere. He had to betray one friend to another. He had to try to prevent the inevitable, though in his heart, he knew he could do nothing.

And he wondered: should I try?

Chapter Thirty

★★★★★★★★

1600.

In the distance the convoy moved like a giant chain drawn through the desert sand by some unseen hand.

Captain Alissa Breen eased back on the throttle of *Scorpion One*, the solar-powered helo-craft designed specifically for the African war against the Marauders. Breen was young, beautiful, with dark hair and eyes, a veteran of the African war. Only her mission had changed.

Now that the war with the Marauders was over, the aircraft was being utilized in a reconnaissance mode. This meant there were no smart bombs aboard the ship, nor were there any uranium-depleted bullets in the ammunition well of the 30-mm cannons.

She was merely assigned to low-level flight, watching for the migration of vultures and the habitations of nomads. She had seen neither in her eight-hour patrol south of the Alexandria Biosphere.

"Lion squadron leader, this is Scorpion One." She spoke directly to Creighton. "Is your better half available?"

Before Creighton could answer, Silver came over the radio, excited at hearing the voice of her childhood friend.

Creighton lifted the hatch over his cupola and looked up, spotting the silent ship as Breen cruised in from the north. He heard Silver ask, "Are you going to land?"

Before Breen could answer, Creighton snapped over the radio, "Negative. This isn't an afternoon social. Maintain surveillance Scorpion One. Adjust your line of patrol to the west. I see smoke on the horizon."

Breen had seen the smoke before making radio contact. She chose to contact Creighton, figuring he would send an IFV to investigate. She was given specific orders on her patrol: find the convoy and stay close.

"Negative, Lion leader. I'm to hook up with you and provide convoy assistance. Adjust your course forty-five degrees to the northwest. There is a deep depression three miles to your front. That'll slow those gas-guzzlers to a crawl."

"Thanks for the information. But I would appreciate your checking out the smoke. There may be nomads. If so, we need to determine if we can be of assistance."

Breen banked hard right. Moments later she was over the smoke.

"My God," she whispered over the radio. "There must be hundreds of vultures swarming over what appears to be seventy or eighty bodies."

Creighton flipped the switch of his radio to internal net. "Reno, check out the situation. If there's any survivors, bring them in. Kill all the vultures."

Falken's IFV raced toward the rising column of smoke. When he reached the source of smoke, he saw several buzzards had been killed, stripped of feathers, and were roasting over the fire. The carcasses were burned black. Around the fire lay the remnants of a nomad group; all were dead. Vultures were feeding on the bodies.

He saw a group of four buzzards attack a single body; within seconds the body was rendered to nothing but a skeletal reminder of its form.

"Start shooting," Falken ordered.

The troops in his IFV, dressed in SIPE suits, dismounted and began shooting the vultures. The weapons made little noise because of sound suppressors on the muzzles; there was only a slight emission of smoke from the weapons. The black figures fell from the sky, targeted perfectly by the sighting sensors that made inaccuracy virtually impossible. Finally the vultures were either dead or in flight.

That was when Falken heard the distinct voice of a baby crying. Racing toward a pile of rocks, he found a small child lying beneath the sand, only its face visible. Nearby, the child's mother lay nearly consumed.

Falken dug the child out of the sand and walked back to his IFV.

★★★★★★★★★★★★★
Chapter Thirty-one
★★★★★★★

Colt Derider descended from a long line of adventurous Americans; Americans who enjoyed building things, not blowing things up. Derider was an engineer; on his personnel file the background information summarized his life as the following: engineer, surface transportation, locomotive (electric and/or solar powered).

How he wound up in Quadrant One, Africa, began two years before. He was transferred from DesFor, Western Quadrant of the United States, where he had just completed building a railroad from the Omaha Biosphere to the Vegas Biosphere, via Salt Lake and Carson.

Like his forefathers, Derider loved trains, especially the old steam locomotives, though outdated and no longer considered in any sense other than historical. Visions still filled his head of his ancestors: Parren Derider, the surveyor for Grenville Dodge during the 1800s when Dodge was building the Transcontinental Railroad. Or Parren's son, Colt, his namesake, who carved the trail through the steaming jungle of Panama, linking the two great oceans before the building of the Panama Canal.

Tough, hearty men. Men who faced danger, like Nick Ruhland, the chief engineer aboard the train code-named Marge. Ruhland was a big man with dark hair and eyes, and huge hands; hands that moved smoothly, even gently over the computer keyboard. Like Derider, his world was the world of trains. He had driven the first train from the Omaha Biosphere to Reno on its initial shakedown run. Given the opportunity to bring the train to Africa, he volunteered immediately. The journey across the ocean was the worst; he was seasick most of the time, but survived by keeping his thoughts centered on his duty.

Marge was now parked outside the Alexandria biosphere. The engine was bullet-shaped; on the sides were weapons platforms integrated into the hull. On the nose, another weapons system could pop out from its concealed station. The weapons were mostly rockets, with the exception of the nose system. The nose weapons platform was a .30-mm six-barreled chain gun. The uranium depleted bullets were armor piercing and could reduce a tank to scrap metal in an instant.

Trailing in tandem behind the main engine were several fortress cars, heavily armed platforms that provided flank protection to the train. Included in the string of platforms were a mess car and a hospital car where surgery could be performed.

The most impressive platform was what Ruhland called the "hunter" platform. The platform was armed with multiple-warhead heat-seeking missiles capable of being launched, seeking a target based on a computer image, and either killing the target acquisitioned, or if no target was found, returning to the launch platform where the missiles could be recovered, rearmed if necessary, and redeployed.

From other cars IFVs could be loaded and deployed down ramps. More than a dozen cars were designed to deploy MBTs. And there were four cars designated as the armory.

The rear car was not a caboose, the traditional work car of the train. Instead, there was an exact replica of the front engine compartment, complete with weapons system. The train could fight in either of two forward directions while putting out full fire suppression on the flanks from the platforms.

The train arrived prepared to fight. The only obstacle was the track bed. Track bed had to be laid in whatever direction the train was deployed. The process of raising and grading the bed, which rose four feet from the surface, laying cross ties, then laying and joining track, was done by one autonomous unit affectionately called "Roadbed Ruthie."

Ruthie was a large contraption that moved across the surface, gouging up sand, which was then conveyed through a heat compactor that literally turned the sand into liquid. The liquid sand was mixed with a rapid-cooling chemical, then channeled into the pouring groove at the center of the machine. Once the liquid was poured, the setting process followed almost instantly; however, before the cooling process was complete, cross ties were implanted into the planed surface. The next step was the placement of interlocking tracks onto the ties.

Track was laid at the rate of five miles per hour— track that would never have to be repaired. Electronic sensors in the tracks picked up body heat, differentiating humans from animals, and was self-protecting, capable of electrocuting saboteurs.

Like a giant snail leaving its slimy trail across the earth, Ruthie had left her signature from the west coast of Africa to near the banks of the Nile.

Only one addition had been made since the train's arrival on the continent. Seismic equipment now gave the engineers the means to examine the subsurface, detecting movement from the now-fragile shell of earth since the Cataclysm.

Ruhland had been trained in this technique and constantly remained updated on any disturbance beneath the surface.

He had just returned from a trip carrying survivors of the Alexandria Biosphere to an outpost of the Eastern Quadrant when he ran a computer check on the seismic equipment.

His eyes widened as he picked up a microphone and called Colonel Clayton. "We may have encountered another problem, Colonel."

Clayton had slept little in the last few days. Problems seemed to arise like foul odor from a murky swamp. "What now?"

Clayton listened as Ruhland explained what the equipment had detected. "Are you certain of this, Mr. Ruhland?"

"Damn certain."

"How long?'

"If my calculations are correct, there may be no more than three hours."

Clayton looked at his watch. "Damn. Not enough time."

"Then you better tell them to hurry."

Clayton broke off the contact and quickly called Major Creighton. "You best keep moving, Major. Seismic data indicate you're traveling through a zone that will soon be struck by an earthquake!"

Chapter Thirty-two

"What next?" Puhaly mumbled. He had listened to TC explain the situation. They knew there was only one chance: a flat-out run to the north. According to the calculations given him by Ruhland, Clayton informed TC the convoy was sitting at the epicenter of an earthquake that could reach eight points on the Richter scale.

The word traveled quickly through the convoy: time was now of the essence. There would be no stopping for any reason whatever.

In a secured IFV, Benhaddou had heard the soldiers talking of the earthquake. His mind began to formulate a plan. He could only hope that Magbe and his close supporters were thinking the same thoughts: the discussion they had had before he surrendered to Creighton.

Benhaddou was no stranger to earthquakes. He had experienced many while living in the north of Africa. The drastic loss of water beneath the earth's surface during the Cataclysm had weakened the earth's crust. He had seen entire areas suddenly become deep depressions in the earth; cracks ran for miles and were often hundreds of meters in breadth.

He closed his eyes and waited.

In another IFV, Magbe sat across from Abu. The two men sensed there was something changing in their favor by what was happening. They spoke to each other in their arabic language, to the ignorance of the guards.

"You should not have trusted Benhaddou," said Abu. "He has betrayed us."

Magbe smiled and said nothing for a moment. "There is something you have forgotten, my friend."

"Which is?"

"Amina. And the others."

The Hakama's instructions had been followed to the letter. Benhaddou knew there was no escape once he learned of the explosion. He and Magbe had decided surrender would buy them time. The convoy would be moving away from the blast zone toward safety. Somewhere along the way there would be the opportunity for escape. Both agreed the woman of Creighton's would save their lives.

Amina had agreed. She had dismounted from the second tank and made a hurried return to the biosphere, arriving in time before the departure. She quickly mingled in with the others, and was now riding aboard one of the transports with two dozen other followers.

Four soldiers were in the rear of the transport; all were young except one man, a veteran of the long war in Africa. He had removed his helmet and closed his eyes, like a veteran, knowing that sleep was often where you found it and wasn't to be ignored.

He had confidence in the three younger soldiers. He pushed his kepi down over his eyes and stretched out his legs. In a matter of moments he was asleep. The transport ambled on, riding over a thin crust of earth that was beginning to waken from the ripple of activity several thousand feet deep.

★★★★★★★★★★★★
Chapter Thirty-three
★★★★★★★

1900.

In Scorpion One, captain Alissa Breen had maintained airborne surveillance, watching through the infrared sensors and thermal imaging of the column. They were moving at a rapid pace, following her guidance instructions as she reconnoitered the forward route. She could see the depression in the distance, then what appeared to be nothing more than an outcropping of rocks that stood in the path of the column. There was a pass through the rocky terrain. She conveyed the report to Creighton through her computer.

Creighton studied the image on his screen. The one thing a tank commander wanted little or nothing to do with was mountain passes. It was too easy to become trapped, or fall victim to avalanche.

"We're not going through there, are we, TC?" asked Puhaly. He feared no man on earth, but an avalanche was something altogether different.

"We have no choice," replied Creighton.

"How far are we from the biosphere?" asked Silver. She was riding in the fold-down jumpseat situated behind Puhaly.

"Twenty miles. The train's waiting." He looked

down at her. Her face glowed in the magenta light painting the interior a pale pink.

"Shit," cursed Puhaly. "These damn Egyptian transports are slowing us to a crawl. We could make twenty miles in fifteen minutes. Why don't we just leave the treacherous bastards and run flat out?"

Creighton smiled. "I've thought about that. But that's not our mission. We all go together."

Puhaly started to argue further. Then he felt the ground shake. The shaking was followed by what he could only describe as riding on a wave. Through the vision block, he could see the moonlit earth suddenly rise and fall. Everything became a blur.

"Jesus Christ!" the gunner muttered. That was when he suddenly felt the MBT rise, then roll onto its back.

Chapter Thirty-four

The ground rose and fell, undulating as if some gigantic snake were moving through the earth's bowels. Rock formations suddenly appeared where moments before there was flat ground. Older formations, standing moments before like darkened ghouls in the desert night, suddenly disappeared, swallowed by the deep trench that now carved its long path through the desert.

The terrible ordeal, the reshaping of earth, took only a few seconds, but it seemed an eternity locked in the convoluting throes of the transmogrifying desert. From the depths of the split that now left its mark on the earth, dust rose in such a torrential storm that all visibility was lost. The rumbling seemed as though it would never stop. Huge boulders, hidden beneath the surface only moments before, were unlocked from their earthen vault and cascaded down the edge of the split, crushing all vehicles and humans in their path.

Two transports seemed suddenly to drop from view as though made to disappear by a magician's hand. The clatter of the twisting steel echoed off the sides of the cavern, mixing with the screams of those ejected from their vehicles.

COBRA CURSE 119

Overhead, in *Scorpion One*, Captain Breen stared in horror at the cloud of dust now billowing upward in excess of two thousand feet. "My God," she whispered, breathlessly, "they're gone."

In Alexandria, Colonel Clayton had moved his command post to the train. He was sitting beside Ruhland, watching the dust cloud now painted red by the infrared camera from the aircraft.

Silence fell like a heavy veil over the train. Colt Derider sat speechless, watching nature rise up and vent her fury. In all his life, he could not imagine anything so sudden, so powerful.

"Those poor people," said Roman. He, too, was breathless. He finally lowered himself into a chair and exhaled heavily. He looked at Clayton. "What are we to do, Thomas?"

Clayton said nothing. He quickly calculated the loss in men and material. He then calculated the personal loss: a son, a daughter-in-law, and an unborn grandchild. It was almost more than he could fathom. That was when he clenched his fists; he couldn't fold up now. This was a crisis. There would be survivors. And the bomb would be launched in five hours.

Clayton stood and walked to the electronic map of the region. The Alexandria Biosphere had been evacuated. The epicenter of the earthquake lay to the south. He started to speak, when suddenly, he heard Derider shout, "Hold on. Here comes the aftershock!"

Clayton felt his legs grow weak. The floor shook, the lights on the map blinked crazily, the train seemed to rise up and return to earth. All the people in the forward control car were thrown from their chairs. Derider smashed his head against the steel bulkhead and lay unconscious. Crawling like a wounded animal, Roman reached the young engineer and cradled his head. With his toga he began stanching the blood flowing from a deep cut over his eye.

Roman looked up at Clayton. "What, Thomas? What are you going to do?"

Clayton looked at Ruhland. "Is this vehicle still operational?"

Ruhland ran a quick computer check. "There's a few springs loose, but no real damage. The threat is from more aftershocks."

"How many more?"

Ruhland shrugged. "One. Ten. Maybe none. I can't tell you what nature has in store."

"Can you pull this train back to a safe zone? Away from the blast area?"

Ruhland checked the map. "That's one hundred and seventy-five miles. If there's no systems damage I can make that in forty-five minutes."

Again Clayton looked at the map. "How fast will this vehicle really travel? I mean with everything shoved to the limits?"

Ruhland didn't have to think. "Seven hundred miles an hour. Faster than the speed of sound."

Clayton again looked at the map. "You say that track-laying contraption of yours lays track at five miles an hour?"

Ruhland grew suspicious; his voice was cautious. "Yes, sir. Why?"

Clayton tapped the area of the earthquake. "We do this in a three-step fashion. First, I'll take a patrol to Creighton's location. Police up the casualties. Find survivors—if there are any. You take the train out of harm's way and be ready to roll on a moment's notice in my direction at full speed."

He looked at Derider, who was stunned but coming out of the pain well enough to understand Clayton's direct orders. "Meanwhile, your track-laying contraption starts laying track. Right now. You have the track laid directly toward Creighton's location. I'll be waiting. If I think there's time, you come running like a bat out of hell. If you get there in time, I'll send for the train. We'll load and run for the safe zone."

Roman looked incredulously at Clayton. "That's insane. You'll never reach them in time. You don't have any vehicles that can cross that terrain. You've sent all your equipment to the safe zone."

Clayton laughed and wore a crazy look on his face. "Not quite. I've still got the *Sea Stallion*. She can move across sand. Sand is like an ocean, just a little firmer!"

PART FOUR: PURGATORY

★★★★★★★★★★★★★
Chapter Thirty-five
★★★★★★★★

Major Abraham Creighton had the distinct feeling that he was sitting upright, though at something of an angle. He was harnessed into his seat when the earthquake struck. His head was protected by his helmet. He concluded it was as though his tank had taken a direct hit from another MBT. That wasn't the case; there was no fire.

The sensation could only mean one thing: he was buried beneath the earth. He had done this intentionally in previous patrols, either to conceal his vehicle from an enemy, or in following a desert storm that buried the MBT beneath tons of sand.

He was staring through the vision block. There was no sky; no stars. There was only blackness. It was as though he were in a sarcophagus.

He heard a moan in the darkness. The shock had knocked out the interior lights. He reached for the auxiliary and flipped the switch. The inside of the MBT suddenly turned a bright white. He looked around.

"Jesus." He could see his wife. She was lying on her back at the bottom of the tank. He glanced to his gunner. "Steve. You all right?"

There was no response; then, a slow groan issued

from Puhaly's bleeding mouth. "What the hell happened?"

"We dropped through the opening." He looked past Puhaly's feet. "Check on Fergus."

Puhaly slowly pulled himself from his seat and reached down to the driver. There was silence, then a muffled cry. "He's dead, TC. Little fella's neck snapped."

Creighton felt the pain shoot through his body. He had known Fergus Felt since childhood. He had been Creighton's only driver. "What about Silver?"

Puhaly crawled to her crumpled form. "She's breathing." He reached to a locker in the bulkhead and removed a canister of water. He gently poured the water onto her forehead. Moments later, her eyes slowly flickered open.

Silver slowly moved her muscles and limbs, starting with her toes and working toward her shoulders. When she was certain no bones had been broken, she pulled herself onto her knees. She, too, had a cut over her eye. "I'm not hurt."

"Steve, check your hatch. Mine is locked tight."

Puhaly reached for his hatch and gave a jerk on the opening lever. "Nothing. Tight as a fat woman's stockings."

"Check the emergency escape hatch." He watched as Puhaly went to the floor of the tank and turned the lever.

The lever cleared, but the hatch opened only inches. "Damn. We're locked into this bitch. I figure we're buried. Maybe we can drive out."

Creighton shook his head. "Drive where? We might be sitting a few feet inside a ledge. I've fallen all I care to inside this bucket."

"What then? Sit here and mummify?"

"I've got an idea. You won't like it. It's risky."
"Your plans generally are. What you got in mind?"
"Load an HE round into the cannon."
"What!"
"You heard me: load an HE round into the cannon. It's the best I can come up with. We'll see if high explosives can blow some of this debris off the hull."

★★★★★★★★★★★★★

Chapter Thirty-six

★★★★★★★★

2030.

Colonel Thomas Clayton had no sooner climbed aboard the bridge of the *Sea Stallion* when he shouted, "Move her out. Full speed!"

Captain Bruce Wills was offshore from the end of the track when he received the call from Clayton. His craft had been stationed there to monitor the radiation and collect other data from the incoming neutron weapon. After confirming Clayton's assessment, that the hovercraft could travel over sand, though not as fast as over water, he came ashore and drove the craft almost to the bullet-nose of the train.

Clayton took the microphone. "Scorpion One . . . are you in contact with any of the ground personnel at the earthquake site?"

There was a long pause, then Breen's voice replied, "I've made contact with Captain Falken. He and a few units survived. There's no word on Creighton. The dust is clearing, and I can now go down and make a visual for you."

"Put it on camera. I want to see what's happening."

Wills turned on the television, and for the first time they saw the aftermath of the quake.

"Mother in heaven," whispered Roman. Clayton said nothing. He stared in silence at the site.

A long split ran north and south, measuring more than four miles. At the center of the split the earth had parted nearly five hundred yards.

"Are you getting this, Derider?" asked Clayton over the mike.

Derider had volunteered to ramrod the Roadbed Ruthie phase of the operation. He was about to begin laying the first of new roadbed and track when Clayton's voice came over the net. "Yes, sir. It's a helluva hole. Ask the pilot to fly in our direction. I want to get a look at the terrain we'll be crossing."

Breen flew toward the Alexandria Biosphere. From what Derider could make of the desert there appeared no topographical problems along the proposed rescue route. There was just a single spire rising from the end of the deep trench, a promontory of rock.

"Well?" snapped Clayton's voice.

"I'll aim for that promontory. Have your people there in four hours," replied Derider.

Clayton keyed the mike. "Make it in three hours." He looked at Wills. "Steady as she goes, Captain."

Then he looked back at the screen. He heard Breen's voice. "I've spotted a survivor on foot. It appears to be a man."

The camera picked up the image of a lone man standing at the edge of the great split. He appeared to be relieving his bladder into the black hole.

Clayton didn't need further identification. He could tell his identity by the man's stature and the contemptuous act.

"Benhaddou!"

★★★★★★★★★★★★
Chapter Thirty-seven
★★★★★★★★

Reno Falken was on the opposite side of the fissure when he spotted Benhaddou. He was looking through his Starlight binoculars, searching for survivors, when he saw the shape of a man emerging along the crevasse. The second he recognized Benhaddou he pulled his pistol and fired three shots. He missed. That's when he heard a groan from behind and saw another man coming at him. He recognized the man called Abu. His clothes were torn; his face was dripping with blood.

Abu was charging, carrying a heavy rock over his head. Falken raised his pistol and fired into Abu's chest. The man pitched back; the rock dropped onto his face with a disgusting crunch.

Swerving, he saw two more people. The man called Magbe and the woman Amina had joined with Benhaddou on the other side of the fissure.

That's when he heard the muffled sound, followed seconds later by a heavy blast coming from about twenty feet below the edge of the fissure on the opposite side.

A red tongue of flame shot through from inside the earth; then another roar of the cannon followed as more debris was blasted away.

Looking directly at the hole, which was facing out into the openness of the fissure, Falken could make out the remnants of a cannon. The barrel was now ripped apart at the business end, but there was no fire or smoke coming from the vehicle.

Falken held his breath, wondering who the survivors were, and how they would survive reaching the ledge.

★★★★★★★★★★★★
Chapter Thirty-eight
★★★★★★★★

"We did it, TC! We fuckin' well did it!" shouted Puhaly.

"Don't start celebrating. We still have to get out of this mess. Grab the weapons, and the EV packs. I'll check out the outside. Silver, move easy. We still don't know what we're up against."

Creighton could see through the vision block. He could see the light from the high power floodlight of *Scorpion One.* He could also see that they were literally on the edge of the crevasse.

"Quick, Steve. Give me a hand-held communicator."

Puhaly reached into the EV—escape and evasion—rucksack and took out a small hand-held communicator. "Scorpion One . . . this is Lion leader. Request assistance."

Creighton quickly explained his plan.

Breen responded, then contacted Falken. Falken was so excited it was Creighton that he nearly fell over the ledge.

"I'll be ready when you arrive on my position," replied Falken. He raced to the rear of his IFV and removed an EV rucksack. He took a heavy rappeling rope from the ruck and charged toward an open area. Seconds later *Scorpion One* hovered over their position. He quickly attached the rope to the skids of the helo and waved at Breen.

Scorpion One lifted off and shot straight across the blackness of the open earth. In seconds she was hovering over Creighton's MBT, the light capturing TC as he knelt on the hull. Carefully she lowered the rope to the waiting tank commander.

"Let's get out. Nice and easy." He reached through the open hatch for Silver and took her hand. Puhaly came up through his hatch. The three reached for the rope and grasped with all their strength.

As the aircraft lifted off, Puhaly looked back and whispered, "So long, Fergus . . . sleep tight, you sweet little shitass."

The downwash from the helo rotors loosened dirt supporting the heavy MBT; then more fell away. Looking down before he neared the edge, Creighton saw Ribald's Chariot slip from its perch and drop into the vast darkness of the open earth.

Chapter Thirty-nine

The desert on Magbe's side of the fissure was strewn with disabled vehicles, and the dead, injured, or merely panicked followers of his cult. It was then that he realized all was lost; that the dream founded before the Cataclysm would not become reality. That God had, in the end, stood in front of the Hakama.

Was it not God who at that moment had opened the earth, leaving the followers to die from the neutron weapon that would soon destroy this part of the world?

He was a man dejected. He was, by the hand of God, a victim of his own cobra curse. His own treachery.

He was, unlike Benhaddou, and Amina for that matter, not a survivor. Not a survivor in the harshness of the world. In the cruelty of the desert.

He saw Benhaddou race to an IFV that was lying on its side. With the help of several dazed followers, the man he thought would be his ally was able to right the vehicle. He shouted for Amina, who followed, bleeding, injured, her visions of great power with Magbe gone.

Magbe was nothing more significant now than any of the scattered boulders lying about the wasteland at the rim of the earthquake's opening. He sat down, lowered his face into the palms of his hands, and wept.

On the other side, Creighton had rounded up the survivors and whatever equipment was still operational. It was when he realized there were not enough vehicles to transport his men, much less the survivors of Magbe's followers, that a familiar voice chimed in over Falken's radio.

Falken was grinning when he handed the microphone to Creighton. "It's your father."

The voice was to the point. "What's your situation?"

Creighton gave what information he had. "Armbrust and Panther squadron were deployed to the flanks, so they were relatively unharmed. The transports were in the center with my squadron running point and rear security. My MBT is out, along with several others. A few survived but the treads were damaged. A lot of casualties inside the units from the impact. Falken's IFV is operational and a few more. For the most part Lion squadron is nonoperational. We've got a lot of seriously wounded personnel."

Creighton paused. "You better get the train moving west. We're not going to make the rendezvous. Not everyone." He looked at Silver. "I'd like to make a personal request."

"What?"

"Request Captain Silver Allenbey be lifted out of the area to your location aboard *Scorpion One*."

There was a pause. "Request denied."

Creighton felt the bile rise in his throat. "You rotten sonofabitch! She's going to have your grandchild!"

Clayton laughed, and Abe thought the man had gone insane. Then he heard the commander of

AfriKorps say, "I'm about six miles from your location aboard *Sea Stallion*. Silver's needed to attend to the wounded. I'm coming to get you, son. So sit tight. I'll be there in ten minutes."

"You can't carry everyone aboard that boat."

"No . . . but the train can."

"The train?"

"Roger. Derider is on his way, laying track like a wild man. When he reaches your location we'll load everyone aboard and set a new land speed record to the safe zone."

Creighton handed the microphone to Falken. "May I use your IFV?"

Falken said nothing. "No . . . but I'll be happy to drive you anywhere you want to go."

★★★★★★★★★★★★
Chapter Forty
★★★★★★★★

Roman Standish couldn't have been more pleased by hearing Colonel Clayton's orders, nor more pleased than what he was now seeing while standing on the bridge of *Sea Stallion*.

"Would you look at that, Roman," said Clayton. He was pointing to the sea of light that spread forward of the bow of the *Sea Stallion*. A lone figure was walking, framed in the light. He seemed to ignore the noise and the presence of the unlikely seacraft floating over the ocean of sand.

Shona paused in his stride when the hovercraft swung to port to avoid drowning him in the hurricane of flying dust being kicked up by the massive turbojets beneath the main deck. The captain didn't stop but merely slowed while Roman ran to the rail and motioned to Shona. A rope was dropped over the starboard rail and the nomadic warrior pulled himself aboard.

"You beautiful . . . insane . . . madman!" yelped Roman. He couldn't have appeared happier to be holding his newborn child.

Shona was covered with dust, yet he retained a sense of elegance. He was tired, his robe soaked with sweat, but there was a strength in his eyes that said he could have gone farther, alone if necessary, to complete his mission.

Brought to the bridge and given water, he listened to Roman explain the earthquake, its aftermath, and the deadly timetable they were up against.

"Then Benhaddou survived."

"At this point. I wouldn't doubt if there were significant others in pursuit."

"Abraham?"

"We heard him talking moments ago to Captain Armbrust from Falken's IFV. He's in pursuit."

"It will be dangerous."

Roman smiled cherubicly. "Major Creighton is a dangerous man. So are Falken and Puhaly. I believe they have the necessary resources to recover the escaped prisoner."

Shona laced his fingers together. He was in deep thought when he asked, "And then what will they do?'

"Return him to prison. Of course."

"Of course." Shona's voice seemed to trail off.

Clayton added to the drama. "Scorpion One's on his ass, giving Creighton directional assistance. She has the solar signature locked up in her heat-seeking equipment. They'll ride that bastard to the ground."

"What about time."

"Humph." Clayton grumped. "That brother of yours is no fool. He knows which way the wind blows—and which direction is the safe zone. That's where he's heading. We'll corral him—either in the desert, or in the safe zone. Or blow his ass to kingdom come!"

"Benhaddou is a wary and great adversary. He will not give up easily. I suspect he has plans that might surprise you," added Shona.

Roman studied him for a moment. "How did you expect to find him?"

Shona shrugged. "I expected to find the convoy. Then I was going to kill my brother. That would be best for all. Now he may escape."

"Not on your life." Clayton was pointing out the window of the bridge. Two sets of headlights were seen jumping herky-jerky through the darkness.

"Creighton's on him. It's a matter of time." He keyed the mike. "You got him, Abe. Blow his ass away."

Before Abe could respond—or fire—the radio from the IFV driven by Benhaddou suddenly joined the commo net. "I would not fire, Colonel. There is something you should hear."

The distinctive sound of a baby's cry came over the radio.

Then Creighton's voice could be heard, telling Clayton, "The sonofabitch has the IFV that was carrying the baby we discovered at the nomad camp. I can't fire without killing the baby, Colonel."

Clayton thought for a moment. "Break off pursuit and return to the earthquake site. We have more important things to do. There'll be another time." Then to Benhaddou he said, "Nothing better happen to that baby. We're tracking your every move. I am giving you permission to proceed to the safe zone. I am issuing orders that you are not to be harmed. If you turn over the child to one of our patrols you'll be given twenty-four hours' reprieve. Is that a deal?"

Benhaddou's laughter filled the bridge of *Sea Stallion*. "I suspected as much."

"Captain Wills . . . proceed to the crevasse."

Wills gave the order and the *Sea Stallion* roared

away. In the distance, he could see Creighton break off the pursuit. He looked at Shona. "We'll get him. Eventually. He only has one way to go from here."

Shona didn't look convinced.

Ten minutes later the arrival of the *Sea Stallion* was both welcomed and regretted by Creighton. In both senses of the word he had lost most of his patrol, the first time he had experienced such a loss. He had also lost the opportunity to kill Benhaddou. Which loss was the greater he wasn't certain of when he approached Clayton and saluted.

The colonel clapped him on the shoulder and said, "Show me the situation." Then he checked his watch. "I hope Derider's pushing that contraption to the limits."

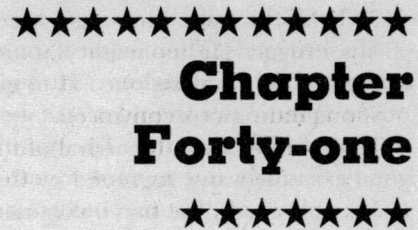

Chapter Forty-one

2130.

Colt Derider had pushed Roadbed Ruthie to her limits. Every digital gauge was reading in the red when he received his most recent call from Clayton. The engineer could only assure him that he had made six miles in the last hour.

"That's not good enough. You won't be giving me a margin of safety. We need that train at this end on my schedule. So listen young man, I don't care if you have to nurse that bitch or walk in front with a pick and shovel to speed up the process. You have two hours. I'm sending for the train at precisely twenty-two hundred hours. You have the track laid to my position or get ready for that flying locomotive to plow right through your young ass!"

Clayton looked at Abe with a grin. "He's a good man. He just needs a little motivation. Now, show me the wounded and what's left of this disaster."

Silver had set up a temporary shelter for the injured. The dead were piled into an area near the lip of the crevasse.

"I'm nearly out of medical supplies," she told him.

"There'll be plenty of supplies on the train. Make do with what you have, Captain."

"What if the train doesn't get here?"

He shrugged. "Then medical supplies won't matter, now will they . . . daughter." He smiled, and reached out to squeeze her shoulder with gentleness. Then he whispered, "Don't worry. The train will get here. I've got a grandbaby due in a few months."

He walked off, but he couldn't help but wonder if he had made the right decision.

He knew, however, that where Silver and his grandchild were concerned, the subject was moot: Silver would leave in *Scorpion One* if the train didn't reach their location in time.

He motioned for Creighton. They walked to the edge of the crevasse.

Creighton asked, "Colonel, just what are we up against with this blast?"

Clayton pointed to the southwest. "The missile will detonate at approximately 2400 hours over or near the Cairo Biosphere. The initial blast will extend for approximately twenty-five miles. That's the area in which nothing will be left standing. Only a deep hole will exist. Extension into the next area will be proceeded by Hell's own fire. A wall of fire, the firestorm. Beyond that range, the blast will continue like a raging hurricane, and as I understand it, the sand will become like tiny bullets. Behind that will come the radiation. The radiation has a short life, but very deadly to humans and microorganisms. In short, the weapon will kill every living thing that comes into contact for another fifty miles. Theoretically, the radiation will get anything else that is within the next twenty-five miles. Of course, wind will carry some of the radiation beyond the range, but it's a rapidly disintegrating type of radiation, especially designed so that the user can occupy the contested area within a reasonable period of time. Unlike the older nuclear weapons. What does that tell you?"

"That tells me that if the train doesn't arrive in time, we can hole up here, in the MBTs and IFVs, and the fissure can be used as a deep bomb shelter."

Clayton looked down into the darkness. "Not quite. It's doubtful the vehicles could withstand the effects of the blast. The fissure might even become a gigantic landslide."

Creighton looked puzzled. "I don't understand, sir."

Clayton turned to him, his hands clasped to the rear of his back. "Do you concern yourself when your MBTs are caught in a desert sandstorm?"

Creighton thought for a moment. "No, sir."

"What is the first thing you do when you are inundated with sand?"

"Run up the breathing periscope to draw air into the unit and ride out the storm."

"Next step?"

"Once the storm is over, full power and push our way out of the sand."

"Give that some thought before you answer the next question. What do you use in order to avoid chemical or biological contamination?"

A slight smile formed on Creighton's mouth. "I'll be damned. A SIPE suit. We have air, heat-resistant covering, contamination protection, and bulletproof temperance."

"And how do you avoid a blast?"

He looked into the deep cavern. "By shielding your unit from the blast, using terrain, surface structures, or dug-in emplacement."

"Your plan of battle?"

"We dig in, wearing our SIPE suits."

"Correct. Next question: why not use the fissure as a natural bomb shelter?"

Creighton thought for a moment. "For two reasons: the earth in the fissure is sand, and normally unstable for digging horizontal foxholes. Ground movement could occur below the ledge where we would have to dig. Second, the slope of the land is not congruent to the blast. The blast, like the wind, will seek low ground. We could wind up torn to shreds if the blast were to flow down into the fissure."

"Very good. Therefore, where do we dig our positions?"

"Should ground movement occur, we don't want to be on the blast side. We go to leeward. On the west side of the fissure."

"Correct."

Creighton considered one other question. "What about Derider?"

"If Mr. Derider and his men don't get here in time they know what they face. They will do the same thing at their position. It's all we've got at the moment. So, let's get busy."

"No chance of calling this thing off?" asked Creighton.

Clayton smiled. "I talked to the president. He wanted to delay the blast for several more hours, but the scientists said that the loss of our people would be negligible compared to the loss caused if the virus spreads any farther. That includes most of the African continent. Traces have already been found in water supplies further east than we anticipated by this hour."

"I suppose the next question is, how many SIPE suits do we have?'"

Clayton looked at TC. "I'll expect to have that answer from you as soon as possible."

Major Creighton walked off; Clayton peered down into the darkness below.

"This should be interesting," he whispered to the blackness.

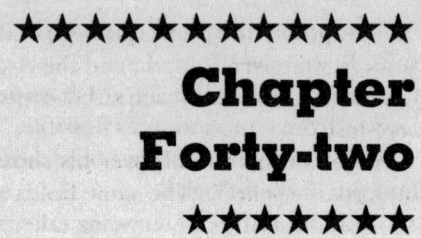

Chapter Forty-two

Biosphere One.

President Woolford Dawson walked through the sparkling sunlight, pausing along the way to spend some time studying the various animals now filling the newly constructed zoo. With him was an entourage of various zoologists, botanists, and biologists, as well as other government officials assigned to the project that would begin replenishing the animal world.

The project had not been easy. Throughout the United States, and the rest of the world, various nations had chosen to assist in the preservation of the animal species all knew would ultimately become lost in the Cataclysm. Nothing could save the animals; only the predators would survive. Even the predators had a rough time as they became game for the surviving human element left in the oblivion beyond the walls of the biospheres.

He paused at a deep pit and watched the emergence of a giant, furry creature. "My God. A polar bear."

The massive creature rose to nearly twelve feet. His giant paws extended toward Dawson. The claws were extended and the teeth bared.

"He looks ready to fight."

"He is ready to fight," added one of the scientists.

"By freezing the sperm and eggs taken from polar bears in northern Canada and the Arctic, none of the genetic survival skills acquired over a million years were lost."

He jerked his thumb over his shoulder toward the deep roar of a lion. "The same holds with the big cats. We had thousands of samples taken from hundreds of prides of lions. They can be reproduced without fear of inbreeding."

"Amazing," Dawson whispered. Then he thought aloud, "I wonder why we didn't think of doing that with mankind?"

The scientists chuckled, not certain what he meant.

Dawson elaborated for his tiny audience. "We've become so cruel. So heartless through the Cataclysm. We give little or no thought to the poor people who suffered outside—or inside—the biospheres. With the outsiders we think only of pacification. With the insiders, we think of re-creating what our ancestors destroyed. Have you given any thought to the millions of people that have been killed by world forces to carry out pacification. In the end, I wonder if we wouldn't have been better off to have just remained outside the biospheres."

One scientist grumped. "That would have been absurd, Mr. President."

Dawson's eyes fell on the polar bear. "Perhaps. But at least we would have all been the same. No one superior group. And we know what that means from history. The superior always try to exert their superiority. It hasn't failed in millions of years of evolution. What makes you think man has been dramatically changed by this nightmare?"

Dawson walked on, toward the roar of the lion. His thoughts went to Africa. To Egypt. The neutron weapon.

Perhaps, he thought again, there should have been no biospheres. At least the entire surviving race would have begun on even footing.

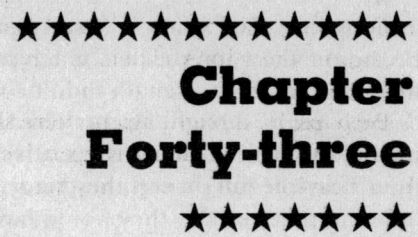

Chapter Forty-three

★★★★★★★★

2200.

Roman found Clayton standing on the western side of the deep crack left by the earthquake. Clayton had ordered the external searchlights from the IFVs and MBTs installed to provide light to begin digging. The lighting had been rigged using cable provided by the *Sea Stallion*. The output wasn't the greatest, yet it did offer enough light to give the soldiers and a handful of Cairo survivors the means to see in order to begin digging individual foxholes into the soft sand. Once the holes were dug, the SIPE suits would be donned and the personnel would climb into their holes and wait for the train:

or wait for the blast!

His plan was simple: let the blast wash over the top of their position. They would more than likely be safe from the firestorm and contamination; it was the hurricane windstorm they had to consider. If his calculations were correct, the deadly storm would pass over their positions.

"This is all quite frightening . . . and quite unsettling, Thomas," said Roman.

Clayton turned and looked at the man he had first met as a young cadet. Roman had taught philosophy in a time when it wasn't really needed. But he taught the young cadets much more. He taught them dignity. That strength didn't come from merely being a great warrior. That strength came from the courage within. From conviction. From listening to their horrible tales when they returned from battle, insisting that one day they would have a normal life.

Clayton loved the old man and had no intention of allowing any harm to come to him.

"I know," he said gently. "But you needn't worry."

"Why? I'm about to put on a strange-looking suit, then be placed in a vertical grave where I'm to wait for a hurricane or firestorm, or whatever it is that's coming. That, to me, is something that warrants worry."

Clayton laughed. "Not at all, Roman."

Roman looked at him warily. "What do you mean?"

Clayton checked his watch. "You don't really think I would risk either the *Sea Stallion* or *Scorpion One* in such a situation, do you?"

"I hadn't given it much thought. My mind has been rather preoccupied with concerns other than your concern for military equipment. Such as my life. And the lives of others."

"I do concern myself with the lives of others. Do you remember what you once called me?"

Roman smiled. "I've come to change my mind on that matter."

"A nihilistic warrior. A soldier who saw nothing moral or immoral about warfare. That war was simply an everyday part of life. That morality didn't enter into the process."

"And you think I was wrong?" He was testing the man for the first time in decades.

"I thought then that you were right."

"And now?"

Clayton smiled. "I've learned from this African experience, Roman. I feel as though there is a morality to warfare. That it's wrong. That it serves nothing good. Even when forced to war."

"Are you becoming a pacifist in your old age?"

Clayton laughed. "No. Just a pragmatist. I'll still fight to stay alive, but I would like a chance first to have at least the *opportunity* to discuss whether it's necessary. Whether it's really important."

Roman stared at the lights. "You're leading up to something, Thomas. We're old friends. Speak what's on your mind."

"Many years ago I made a terrible mistake."

"When you killed the man that Abraham thought was his natural father?"

He shook his head. "No. I could live with that. That was self-defense. I wasn't honest about my love with Abraham's mother. I was afraid that if I revealed that, and our relationship—the fact that I am his father—that my career would have been ruined. People would have believed that I had killed a great hero to satisfy my personal needs."

"She chose to support you. She chose the same course. To remain silent. Celibate. And why? Because she knew that without your career . . . you would not have remained the same man that you were. That you've become. She knew that the love she had for you—and you for her—would have ultimately destroyed you both in any event."

He took a deep breath. "You always know the right things to say."

"I'm a philosopher. I'm supposed to know the right things to say."

He gripped the old man by the shoulders. "And I'm the military commander of AfriKorps. Which means my orders are to be followed to the letter, without exception."

"Correct. And I suppose next you'll order me into that infernal hole now that I've agreed to your omnipotence."

"No, old friend. I order you away from danger. I order you to board the *Sea Stallion* and return to the coast and put to sea with Captain Wills. The ride will be a little bumpy when the dissipating winds hit the coast, but your chances there are much better than here. Besides, you'll only get in the way."

Roman's eyes suddenly filled with tears. "It's more than that, isn't it, Thomas?"

He nodded. "Yes. I want you to take Silver with you. If anything happens to Abe, she'll need someone to help with the child."

"What about you? You might survive."

"I wouldn't want to survive, old friend, even if I thought it possible."

"When do we leave?"

"In five minutes."

"Does Abraham know?"

"Not yet."

"Is there any way possible that he might go?"

Clayton shook his head. "He's needed here. I'll need him if any of us are to survive."

"And may I ask one favor?"

"What's that?"

"Would you order Shona to accompany us?"

"Consider it done."

They shook hands. Then Clayton returned to his duty and Roman returned to his.

Chapter Forty-four

Clayton walked directly to where a group of infantrymen were digging in the sand. He motioned to the leader. "Captain Falken." Clayton stepped into the darkness and watched Reno approach. Reno was the best ground soldier he had ever known. The best tracker, manhunter, and desert guerrilla in Africa. He was what was called a desert rat.

"Yes, sir." Reno saluted.

"I have a mission for you, son." He walked off with Falken, toward *Scorpion One*, explaining what he had in mind.

Falken listened and accepted the mission with mixed emotions. "One part of me wants to thank you . . . the other part wants to request permission to deny."

"I understand. But I think it's important enough. You might say we're hedging our bets."

"Yes, sir. It's why you made the agreement?"

"That's right. I don't know what's going to happen here. We can't get our personnel out of here with no vehicles, and the *Sea Stallion* can only carry limited weight since it's on sand and not water. Do you understand what you're to do?"

"Yes, sir. Have you contacted the train?"

"I'll do that momentarily. Remember your orders. You do as I've instructed and nothing else. Is that clear?'

"Clear, sir." He saluted and went to where his gear was stacked. Then he walked to *Scorpion One* and spoke with Captain Breen.

Clayton walked away grinning and saying aloud to some unseen entity, "All right, you bastard, let's see how you like the word of Colonel Thomas Clayton."

PART FIVE: DESERT STORMS

Chapter Forty-five

2230.

Puhaly's powerful muscles worked the fold-out entrenching tool with the ease of a giant earth-moving shovel. He appeared to be driven, and under the dim light beads of sweat trickled down his face onto his shoulders. With each thrust into the ground he was seeing the face of Benhaddou, which made the task easier. Chores such as this never bothered him in the past. He always had his little nemesis Fergus along to chide him and return his own quips, allowing each other to forget the danger.

Fergus was dead. A neutron bomb was about to land no more than fifty miles from their location, and they had no transportation out of the area.

The whir of the *Sea Stallion*'s massive turboengines ruptured the uneasy stillness that had quickly settled, like the realization that in a matter of two hours they might all be dead.

Again Puhaly drove the entrenching tool into the desert sand. He threw the sand forward, building a wall in the direction the blast would come from.

"Like trying to kick an elephant's ass with a rifle stock." His voice filtered over to where Creighton was standing, watching the survivors of Cairo work alongside the AfriKorps survivors.

Creighton turned to see Clayton and Silver approach. Roman was with them.

Creighton saluted. Clayton went directly to the point of the matter. "I'm ordering the *Sea Stallion* to a safe station offshore. Roman and Silver are ordered to board the craft and accompany Captain Wills and his crew."

A broad grin cracked the crusty sand mask covering Creighton's face. He looked at Clayton. "Thank you, sir. May we be excused?"

"You've got five minutes. Don't let her miss her boat." Roman reached over to Creighton. "Good luck, my boy. I'll see you in the morning."

They shook hands. Creighton said nothing. He merely nodded and gripped the philosopher's hand fondly.

Abe and Silver walked toward the hovercraft. Shona was standing on the bow; his arm rose, he waved his spear and called, "Farewell, my friend."

Creighton checked his watch. "Derider should be here soon. But, by God I'm glad you're getting out of here now. It's going to be hectic as hell."

She stepped into his arms and they kissed long and soft. When their faces separated she had the shiny sparkle of sand on her cheeks. He patted the sand away softly, then kissed her again.

They didn't speak of death; or of never seeing each other again. He simply whispered, "I love you. Take care of the baby."

She nodded. She was a soldier; a soldier's wife. A veteran of the war in Africa, she understood that tomorrow might never come. Not for Abraham Creighton.

He walked her to the bow of the *Sea Stallion* and watched her walk up to the quarterdeck. He couldn't help but notice how truly lovely she was; more so than he had ever noticed before.

Then he walked back to where Puhaly continued to dig. He took his entrenching tool and drove the sharp point into the sand. With each thrust he felt the shock of the impact race up his arms into his shoulders.

Then there was the sound of the *Sea Stallion*'s power plants revving to higher rpms. There was the sound of the sand and air mixing, churning into the dark night, turning the hot air even hotter. Grittier.

He didn't look up until he felt the pulsation as the craft began to move. The desert seemed to shake as the turbines roared their fury and slowly, the hull rose, fully inflated, and started to move.

Creighton held his breath as he watched the *Sea Stallion*'s power begin to urge to craft forward.

Faster. Faster. Then there was the sound of *Scorpion One* lifting off, and the two craft started north to safety.

Minutes later there was silence. The people left behind stopped their digging. They watched until the lights of the two craft disappeared on the horizon.

They said nothing. There was nothing to say.

There was only the wait: for Derider . . . or the hell of the neutron blast!

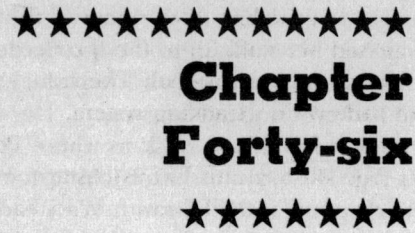

Chapter Forty-six

★★★★★★★★

Nick Ruhland had received the order from Clayton earlier than expected, but he was prepared when the signal came. He gave the verbal orders to the computer and sat back while the train built its speed to blinding proportions. The forward infrared and thermal imaging radar was tracking the terrain, giving him a visual picture of what was to his front. He wasn't looking for an enemy. He was looking to be certain the trackbed had not become another victim of the earthquake.

It was when he switched to the new roadbed being laid by Derider that something caught his eye. He didn't stop the train. That would have been negligent. Instead, he quickly rewound the videotape that constantly filmed to the trains front during a run, until he found what he was searching for.

A single IFV had crossed the tracks only moments before.

He didn't need to wonder who was in it.

It was the IFV that Benhaddou had stolen from the column. The last vehicle, according to Colonel Clayton, that was operational.

He then did what Clayton had instructed him earlier. He pressed a button on the computer switch that sent a signal to the IFVs IFF—Identification Friend or Foe. The signal struck the black-box receiver in the IFV and sent a return signal. The signal was then locked into the train's tracking system. He watched the blip on the screen.

"You bloody murderous bastard. We got you now. Where you go, we'll know your location."

He quickly called Clayton. "Mission accomplished."

Clayton didn't sound especially enthusiastic. When Ruhland heard what he had to say, he understood. "Pick up Derider and his crew, load them aboard the train, and return to your previous station in the safe zone."

"What's happened, Colonel?"

There was a pause, then, "Derider's contraption has broken down. It's irreparable. He's eight miles from this location and that's too far to send even those who can walk to meet you. By the time they got there it would be too late to get your train and the personnel to safety. We'll have to leave the wounded here, including the children from Cairo."

"I'm sorry, Colonel."

"To hell with sorry. Just get that signal transmitted to *Scorpion One*. If I'm going to die I want to know that treacherous bastard won't be far behind."

"Yes, sir." The communication ended.

Ruhland then contacted *Scorpion One*. "Have target locked into tracking system. Prepare to receive microburst."

In the cockpit of *Scorpion One*, Captain Breen turned on a relay computer that would take a passoff from the train's computer. In a split second the burst was complete. Falken's IFV, under the command of Benhaddou, was being tracked by *Scorpion One*.

Breen turned to the seat beside her. "That's a handy invention. Now we can track him without his knowing he's locked up."

From his adjacent seat, Reno Falken flashed an evil grin.

Chapter Forty-seven

2300.

Colt Derider looked like a one-armed man competing in a pole-climbing contest. There was nothing but frustration on his face. He had even thought about kicking Ruthie but knew that would do no good. Besides, it wasn't the machine's fault. She had gotten close. But that only counted in throwing grenades. Not building track.

When the train arrived, beginning its approach ten miles back, he and the crew were waiting. Ruthie would be left to whatever designs the blast had in mind for her.

"What happened?" asked Ruhland.

"Compression conveyer." That was the system that conveyed the sand into the compressor where the sand was liquefied. "Blew completely apart. Damn rotten luck." He stared blankly toward the darkness where the earthquake had ruined the column's chance of a safe rendezvous.

"I'd sure hate to be in their shoes in about an hour."

Ruhland said nothing, except the verbal order. The train sped away, toward the darkness of the safe zone.

Chapter Forty-eight

President Woolford Dawson was not a man to let others assume his responsibilities. He had come to the launch facility with the precise intention of being the sole person responsible for the launching of the missile. He was met at the main gate by Dr. Call and several other scientists involved with the project.

After greeting the president, Call excused himself, saying, "I'll join you in a few minutes, Mr. President."

Dawson thought Call was looking nervous. And why shouldn't he? thought the president.

Dawson knew where the scientist was going. Therefore, he said nothing. Two security guards conducted Dawson to what was called the Red Room. The launch control center. The room was filled with banks of computers; scientists sat at their respective duty stations, all but ignoring the chief executive.

The missile had been transfered from the vault to a launch silo a mile from the facility. The firing sequence had been programmed; all that remained was for two red keys to be turned simultaneously.

Dawson ran through his mind all the minute details that Call had relayed to him over the past twenty-four hours. He was surprised at how easily the scientist had kept everything in layman's terms.

The missile would leave the ground, travel a trajectory that would first track over the Atlantic, then rise through the outer atmosphere, and return to earth. The flight had been estimated at nineteen minutes.

Dawson sipped a cup of herbal tea from a thermos as he watched Dr. Call return. He carried a small metal box. He took a chain from around his neck; on the chain was a tiny key. The doctor carefully inserted the key into a small slot. He opened the box.

Dawson's eyes widened at the sight. Imagine. Two small keys were capable of launching such destruction.

Call carefully inserted the two keys into the slots of the firing mechanism. He was careful, almost to the point of being dramatic. When ready, he stepped back and motioned to the keys.

"Whenever you're ready, Mr. President."

Dawson took a deep breath as he rose from the chair. For a moment he thought he might falter. He found his balance and walked to the two keys. With a firm twist, both keys were turned clockwise 180 degrees.

There was nothing!

Dawson looked puzzled at Call.

Call grinned. "These are not smart missiles, Mr. President."

Before Dawson could respond, there was the feeling of shaking; then a rumble. On the television monitor projecting the launch silo, there was a sudden eruption of the outer silo cover. A huge tongue of flame rose up; white smoke clouded the picture momentarily. The camera panned back, revealing a long cylindrical missile lifting gracefully into the air.

In a matter of seconds the missile was thousands of feet in the air. Seconds later, the missile was out of sight.

The neutron missile was en route to Egypt.

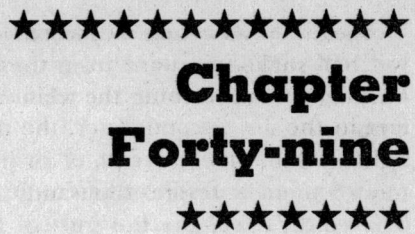

Chapter Forty-nine

★★★★★★★★

2400.

The crescent shape of the moon was brilliant against the black night. There was not a sound, not even the familiar noise of desert night predators. It was, thought Creighton, as though the desert knew that soon a terrible event would occur.

Then there was the voice of Clayton over the hand radio. "*Sea Stallion* is tracking the missile. It's inbound and on target. Don't look in the direction of the blast. Keep your butts down in your holes!"

There were several cries from the Cairo survivors. All wore protective SIPE suits except three, and they were not near the fissure.

Magbe and his three surviving cohorts, Ali, Semir, and Khalil, had fled north into the desert, fearing reprisal from their followers or the AfriKorps. They knew nothing of the time, or even that the missle was nearing the Cairo Biosphere.

They were near the promontory, stumbling through the desert, when they heard a distant rumble. They turned east, toward ancient Mecca, just as the night turned a brilliant liquid white. A huge cloud formed out of the blackness, obscuring the moon, turning the desert white as day.

Then they saw a huge mushroom develop; a gigantic red ball snaked outward from the edges, churning, burning the air, turning the white night into a deep crimson.

They didn't feel the rush of air that was exploding toward them at several thousands of miles an hour. They didn't feel the hot gust of fiery breath that burned over the desert, crystalizing the sand for fifty miles.

They didn't feel the millions of granules of sand that suddenly penetrated the entirety of their bodies, piercing every single pore of their skin.

They didn't feel anything.

They simply dissolved!

★★★★★★★★★★★★★
Chapter Fifty
★★★★★★★★

In his foxhole, Creighton felt the blast of the hurricane wind whip at the exposed opening three feet over his head, spraying the sand with such force he felt he was sitting beneath a giant sand blaster used to reduce concrete to powder. In a sense he was. He couldn't hear the screams of his men; he didn't know if they were screaming.

He heard only the deep, incessant drone of the hurricane wind that was spreading over the desert.

He had known fear in his life. But never the likes of this. He had faced men in battle and overcome his fright not only to fight, but to lead while frightened. To inspire others when you are afraid is one of the greatest challenges a man could face.

But that fear was real. He was facing men of flesh and bone, men of thought and reason. Men of anger and the passion to live. Self-preservation.

This was not an enemy he had known. Not like the darkness, which can be a tank commander's friend. The darkness can cloak a soldier from the enemy, give a canopy of cover to allow rest while the body replenishes its strength.

This was an *unreal* enemy. An enemy he dare not touch or there would be nothing left. An enemy that he could not view; not grasp. Not even shoot at; nor shout at for fear he might be swallowed by the overwhelming force of power being exerted.

This was fright of the type he could never dream of in his worst nightmare.

And worse: it seemed this enemy would never go away. Never withdraw its attack. It was like being caught in a vacuum that left him helpless, and even if he wanted to surrender he could not!

The heat that followed the wind challenged every ounce of technological capability of his SIPE suit. He had turned the unit to full "blow," as the soldiers called the maximum output of the suit. Output that would allow them to run at full speed through 140 degree desert heat and not break a bead of sweat. Now, in the suit, he was drenched in his sweat. He could feel the heat turning his skin into a soggy, mushy mass of tissue that was aching from the intense, incredible heat.

He felt as though he were being microwaved, like a piece of meat in a microwave oven: being cooked from the inside out.

The head-up display on his helmet visor was reflecting a myriad of colors, driving his optical senses wild. It was like wearing contact lenses made of a kaleidoscope of colors. Blue. Red. Green. All the colors of the spectrum, flashing, streaking, stretching into strange and incomprehensible shapes.

All this began to play the mind game on him. He thought for a moment he heard Silver shouting for his help, but his self-discipline, his self-command and control said otherwise.

Then he saw his mother through the head-up display. She was standing beside Clayton. Then she was performing obscene acts with the man he had discovered was his natural father.

Clayton was laughing!

He pointed his weapon and started to fire, but his fingers couldn't close around the trigger. Then he remembered he wasn't holding his rifle!

His whole fucking world was coming unglued while the whole fucking world *was* coming unglued around him!

Then it ended.

★★★★★★★★★★★★
Chapter Fifty-one
★★★★★★★★

Fifty miles off the coast of Alexandria, *Sea Stallion* was faced directly into the wind when the first effects of the blast reached their position. Through the window of the bridge the blast could be seen. There was a distant flash, like that of lightning. Then they waited, not knowing how long it would take the expected tidal surge to reach their position.

On shore, when the blast reached the coastline the water was literally reversed in its course. At first there seemed to be a mutual resistance; gradually, the force of the blast began to fold back the incoming tidal force, turning the seawater on a reverse course.

A giant tidal wave formed, the leading edge building to over thirty feet in height.

Aboard the *Sea Stallion*, Captain Wills watched the radar screen. Then he heard his radarman say, with an incredulous voice, "Holy Jesus . . . it must be forty feet high."

Wills shouted his orders. "Strap yourselves in tight. Here it comes!"

Silver, Roman, and Shona, along with the skeleton crew of the *Sea Stallion*, were sitting in upright chairs bolted to the deck. They wore shoulder harnesses and helmets with shatterproof visors covering their faces. On Wills's command they turned their seats 180 degrees away from the blast and stuck regulators into their mouths, giving them air from a self-contained breathing system built into the bulkhead of the hovercraft.

The initial impact of the leading wave washed over the *Sea Stallion*, driving the vessel downward nearly sixty feet. Designed for inundation, the window of the bridge, built from the same resilient polymer glass that had protected biospheres from the Cataclysm, withstood the initial shock and the pressure of depth.

Looking to the port, Silver could see the darkness of the water outside the glass of the lighted bridge. She had the impression of being inside a light bulb that had been cast into a vat of thick oil.

"Oh, heavens," mumbled Roman. His eyes widened as he saw some giant sea creature slam against the glass. The creature, either a whale or giant shark, bounced off the glass and tumbled out of sight.

Shona never could have imagined such an experience in his wildest dreams. He felt the hovercraft slam into something and could only suspect that they had struck bottom. Which they had.

Sitting calmly at the helm, Captain Wills shoved the throttles to full power, engaged the ballast, forcing injected air into the lower hull.

Suddenly, like a cork held and released under water, the hovercraft began rising toward the surface.

The *Sea Stallion* broke the surface, rising like a dolphin, leaping, urging itself by its own design to regain longitudinal stability.

The first effort failed, sending the bow plunging again into the murky sea, now turned black from the darkness and the silt stirred from the bottom.

Again the *Sea Stallion* rode to the depths. Again Wills pumped more ballast. The *Sea Stallion* rose toward the surface—and suddenly—the protective glass gave way.

A powerful, crushing wave swept through the bridge, the force of the water tearing, pulling, pounding the bodies of those trapped in the blackish hell.

Silver felt herself become lightheaded. Breathing from the regulator, she took deep breaths, but found that difficult as the crushing water pressure seemed to squeeze her chest until finally she could not breathe.

Her first reaction was human: to release herself and run!

That would have been suicidal. She fought the most basic human instincts: to race toward the surface.

Sea Stallion broke through the surface, this time barely arcing out of the water, held low by the weight of the water.

Captain Wills reached and hit a water vent that opened up jets that allowed the water to flow out.

The turbos raced, filling the air with a loud roar; the water began receding.

"We made it," Wills said softly. Toward the bow, another set of waves was approaching like tanks on line, charging through the desert. But they were smaller.

The boat bobbed wildly for several minutes, then settled.

Sea Stallion had done what it was designed to do.

★★★★★★★★★★★★★
Chapter Fifty-two
★★★★★★★★

Aboard Scorpion One, Breen had pushed the throttles to the wall, traveling in a straight line outbound over the top of the fleeing IFV driven by Benhaddou. The plan had been simple: cross-reference with the train on the IFV lockup, then track the IFV until thirty minutes before the scheduled launch.

At 2330, Breen was still locked onto the IFV when she reached to the instrument console and flipped a switch marked SDLB—solar deactivation laser beam. Gripping the directional control stick, where the firing mechanism for all her weapons systems was located, she closed her finger around the trigger.

An invisible particle beam joined the two machines momentarily.

Scorpion One continued through the darkness, flying east toward a wadi at the edge of the safe zone.

The IFV stopped dead in its tracks, its solar power killed by an unseen attack.

At the wadi, a low depression in the rugged desert, which was in the direct line of march of the IFV, Breen and Falken landed, dismounted from *Scorpion One,* and raced to the lowest point they could find. There they quickly dug in and waited. They had hand-held communication with Clayton and would know when the blast occurred: if they coudn't see the actual blast, the radio would suddenly be out of commission.

They had waited. Finally, there was a bright light a hundred miles away. They continued to wait. By the time the blast swept through their position there was nothing more than mild winds. That's when Breen and Falken returned to the helo and became airborne.

They climbed into the helo after both Falken and Breen put on their SIPE suits. The *Scorpion* was sealed and therefore safe from radiation; there was little chance there would be radiation at that distance, but Clayton had insisted.

Scorpion One flew east, toward the area where they last saw the IFV.

"There!" Falken saw the IFV appear on the infrared screen. The doors were open. One figure stood alone in the darkness some fifty meters west of the IFV.

"Go to whisper-mode and land thirty meters to the east of the IFV," Falken ordered.

Breen went to whisper-mode; the air fell silent as the sound of the rotors was muffled.

She inched the helo to the ground and switched off the engine.

"Put on your helmet and switch to thermal imaging." Falken ordered.

The two soldiers slipped out of the helo and advanced toward the IFV. What they found was what they expected. The disabled vehicle had been abandoned.

Reno Falken checked out the IFV. He heard a sound, then eased through the driver's side. Then he smiled.

"Come here, Captain Breen." Then he reached through the door and picked the baby up from the seat.

She took the baby. "The baby's alive!" She couldn't contain the excitement in her voice.

"Contact Colonel Clayton, if you can. Tell him the child is all right." He started to walk away.

"Where are you going?" She pulled at the sleeve of his SIPE suit.

"To take care of some unfinished business."

Chapter Fifty-three

1600.

President Dawson was standing at the new arboretum, built only three months before. A walkway was lined with beautiful trees. Flowers seemed to be growing everywhere. It reminded him of the rain forest in the biosphere, where as a young boy he used to sit and ponder the future, not fully certain there would be a future.

He sat on a bench, glanced at his watch, then looked at the sky. He recalled another report he had received earlier that morning from an expedition to the south. The ozone layer over Antarctica was healing quite rapidly. Soon, earth could expect to begin seeing the types of temperatures it had known before the Cataclysm.

He had a meeting later that day with the newly formed National Education Commission. The purpose was to incorporate the national educational system, which had once been exclusively in the domain of the specials, with the needs of the pacified population.

He marveled at the thought. Hated enemies might one day become friends and live in harmony.

The international scene was coming together. Throughout the world the vicious savages were either being subdued or had been defeated. Only a small area of southeast asia still remained volatile. That would be addressed soon.

He thought he knew the man perfectly suited to lead a military contingent into the area and render it peaceful, as he had done in Africa.

Dawson looked up as he saw his secretary approach. He was carrying a communications briefcase.

Dawson took the telephone and listened for a moment. Then he smiled.

He looked at the secretary, then said, "The situation in Egypt is stable. The weapon eliminated the threat."

He stood and walked toward the west, where the sun was starting to set. He felt good.

It was the best feeling he could recall having in his entire life.

Chapter Fifty-four

0800.

The sun was starting to crawl over the eastern horizon; the sounds of the injured rose up from the sand, filling the air with their desperate cries. Colonel Thomas Clayton walked through the ravaged area, counting the dead, which were few; counting the survivors, most of whom were wounded; all were contaminated by the radiation.

He felt himself becoming sick and wondered if the medical units would arrive in time to help those lying around him, hoping and praying for some form of relief.

Then he heard the beat of a helicopter and saw that *Scorpion One* was inbound. He walked as fast as he could to Creighton. "Get your people assembled."

Breen had done as instructed, staying away from the blast site until the preparations for survivors had been set in motion. He took his field glasses and studied the terrain to the north. Tall rooster tails rose into the air, dust from advancing vehicles.

"They're coming," he whispered.

Abe Creighton had been vomiting now and then

for nearly two hours. He was sick, but alive. The SIPE suits had given the survivors a great deal of protection, but all knew that the protection would only last an indefinite period.

Creighton found Puhaly on his knees, retching. "I feel like I'm going to have to get better before I can die, TC."

"You'll get better." He pointed at the rooster tails. "Look!"

"The decontamination unit." Puhaly breathed heavily. He was trying to stand. Creighton lay a gentle hand on his shoulder.

"Take it easy. You just rest."

Creighton walked through the area. It looked like a battle zone. MBTs, disabled before the blast, sat with their paint stripped to the titanium metal. IFVs had been ripped to shreds by the horrific winds, turned on their sides like children's toys caught in a high wind.

He saw *Scorpion One* land and started toward the helo. He reached the helo as Clayton was assisting one of the passengers to the ground.

"Silver!" Creighton whispered.

Silver Allenbey-Creighton hurried toward him. She reached him just as he collapsed. She took a pouch from around her shoulder and removed a syringe. She quickly gave him an intravenous injection. "This will combat the nausea. There's an antitoxin for the radiation as well. You'll feel better in a few minutes. The poison will stop affecting your system."

The convoy arrived in a few minutes. Brought to the end of track by Ruhland, the vehicles had made good time reaching the disaster site.

The survivors were injected with an antitoxin, then herded directly to the decontamination unit that was set up.

The survivors were decontaminated, as was the area, and fed from a mobile mess unit. An hour after their arrival, the medical unit was transporting the wounded to the train, which was waiting ten miles away.

Arriving at the train, Creighton sat in the control unit, where Ruhland was running the final phase of his systems check. Derider was with him.

He looked up to see Clayton enter. Silver was still in the hospital car, tending the wounded.

Clayton slipped into a chair beside Abe.

"You look tired."

Clayton laughed. "You don't look much better."

There was a long silence, then he said, "I haven't had a chance to thank you for shipping Silver out to sea."

Clayton grumped. "From the sound of it I nearly shipped her to the bottom of the sea."

"I know it was a tough decision."

"You know command requires tough decisions. That's why it's called command."

"Still . . . I want to thank you."

"Thanks accepted. Now get some sleep."

Creighton shook his head. "I can't. No more than you can."

Clayton shook his head. "He's a fine soldier. The best light fighter we've got. Don't worry."

"I suppose you're not?"

He shook his head. "No. I'm a commander. I'm not allowed to worry about a single soldier. I have hundreds—thousands—to worry about."

Clayton closed his eyes. He hoped the lie had been convincing.

Chapter Fifty-five

The hunter had become the hunted. Reno Falken understood that as he followed the last set of tracks leading west from the IFV. The tracking had begun as soon as *Scorpion One* had lifted off with the child. The first set of tracks belonged to the woman, he suspected.

He was right. He found Amina sitting in the sand less than a mile from the IFV. She had apparently heard the helo and begun her frantic escape.

Falken found her an hour later. She was exhausted. The beauty he had remembered from Cairo was gone. She looked haggard. She had not worn a SIPE suit, and once she left the protective cocoon of the IFV, residual radiation drifting west had finally caught her.

She was on her belly, vomiting, when Falken found her.

"Please. Help me," she whispered through cracked lips. She had been in the desert heat for hours without water.

Falken knelt. "Where's Benhaddou?"

She looked at him oddly, as though not really understanding the reasoning behind her answer. "He left me."

"That figures. Which way was he going?"

She shook her head. "I don't know. Away. Away from you."

"Does he know I'm following?"

Again the head shook. "He thought we would be safe. Then the vehicle stopped."

Falken stood up. He raised his field glasses. In the distance he could see the dark speck wrapped in the wafting heat waves rising above the desert. He started west.

"Ple—ase!" she screamed. "You're not going to leave me here! Without food! Without water!"

A slight smile etched Falken's mouth. "You left the baby . . . why should you be treated any different!"

Then the hunt began.

Chapter Fifty-six

1200.

The Morocc named Benhaddou had never known such agony. His bowels had loosened hours ago, preceded by the vomiting; then came the stomach cramps. The horrible headaches followed; then came the muscle spasms.

He had crawled to an oasis that was mostly scrub brush and rocks; a small water hole, the water putrid and green, was set in the middle. He crawled on his belly like a snake until he reached the water.

His hands trembled as he scooped the water onto his face. Rolling over, he could see the sun was directly overhead. Dark figures were circling, their shadows drifting in and out of the brightness of the sun.

He laughed. A dying type of laugh. He thought the vultures were all dead. Then he realized that they were. These had drifted in from the west, free of the deadly virus turned loose by that fool Magbe.

His eyes tightened, and for a second he thought he saw his brother Shona, standing on the rocks.

"Impossible," he told himself. His brother could not have followed him.

The figure then moved, dropping from the rocks, approaching.

Benhaddou reached for his pistol. A shot rang out and he felt a searing pain in his stomach. Then a strange, almost alienlike creature was standing over him.

He could see the eyes behind the visor, and recognized the SIPE suit worn by the AfriKorps soldiers at the Cairo Biosphere.

"Who . . ." his voice trailed off.

"Captain Reno Falken. AfriKorps."

Falken kicked Benhaddou's weapon away. Then he stood several meters away, still aware of how Benhaddou could be as deadly as a cobra so long as he breathed.

"Why don't you kill me?"

"That would be murder. I'm not a murderer."

Benhaddou forced a laugh, then retched. Blood issued from his stomach.

"You're suffering from radiation poisoning. You're going to die."

"How long before I die?"

Falken checked his watch. "I figure about three hours. Longer if I'm lucky."

Benhaddou's eyes widened. "Then you must help me."

Falken shook his head. "I have no medical supplies. No water." He looked up at the vultures circling overhead and laughed.

"If you refuse to help me then that is murder." He tried to spit, only blood oozed along his chin.

"Call it what you wish. I can't help you."

Falken knelt in the sand, his weapon trained on the Morocc. How easy, he thought, to kill the bastard. Then he remembered Clayton's orders: make the bastard suffer the most horrible death you can!

He was. He sat quiet, saying nothing, the thermostat of his SIPE suit set to a temperature that was near cold.

Benhaddou then began crawling toward him. That was when a dark shadow apeared over his head. He looked up in time to see the sharp talons, the crooked razor-sharp beak of a vulture slash at his face.

The tissue was flayed open on his neck, revealing a pulsing carotid artery.

He screamed, trying to pull himself to his knees.

Another vulture swept in. Then he heard Falken speak:

"The vultures of today aren't like before the Cataclysm. Those vultures were scavengers. Today's vultures are predators."

That was when a flock flew in; within seconds Benhaddou was covered with the squawking, fighting, clawing creatures. His screams were loud, pitiful, at first. Then the screams receded into a deep moan, followed by a gurgling.

Falken raised his weapon and began firing. The vultures broke from their prey and flew hurriedly into the sky; some perched on the rocks. Waiting. Knowing the feast had not ended.

Falken approached Benhaddou. The Morocc's flesh had been nearly stripped away from his face. He tried to speak but could not. His eyes were blind, and he wasn't certain if they were still in the sockets.

His eyes!

Tearing out the eyes of his victims had been his trademark.

Then he felt Falken's hands on his face. There was a sharp, slicing sting. He felt something in the sockets of his eyes!

Falken stood, holding Benhaddou's eyes in his hand.

"I'll give these to Creighton, you sonofabitch! After what you once did to his wife, he'll be delighted."

Falken walked away. There was a roar of flapping wings. The vultures pounced on Benhaddou.

Falken watched until there was nothing but the skeleton of the Morocc.

Chapter Fifty-seven

Base Camp One. AfriKorps HQ.

Hamp Florens had returned to his farm on the edge of the AfriKorps camp to find the vegetation had flourished in his absence. He had been there the day the neutron weapon exploded, evacuated from the Alexandria Biosphere aboard the train.

He learned there was a cult within the Cairo and Alexandria biospheres. A cult that was now crushed. The members were not arrested; rather, they were treated humanely—with the exception of Anwar el-Riad, who was charged with accessory to murder. The trial would be in a few days.

He was kneeling in a tomato garden when he heard the rotor slap of *Scorpion One* pass overhead. He watched as the helo drifted down and landed at the headquarters.

At headquarters, Reno Falken stepped out of the helo and walked into the air-conditioned building, followed by Captain Breen.

He wasn't wearing his SIPE suit, which was discarded after Breen had picked him up at the oasis two hours earlier.

He was dirty, tired, but walked with an air of confidence into Clayton's office.

Clayton shook hands with him. "Mission accomplished?"

Falken smiled. "Yes, sir. He'll be no more trouble."

At that moment Creighton, Shona, Roman, Armbrust, Puhaly and Silver barged into the office.

They were so delighted to see Falken they didn't bother to knock.

"Settle down, all of you," Clayton barked. The room fell silent.

Clayton picked up a communique that had been waiting when he arrived earlier that morning.

"There's something you should know. AfriKorps has been ordered to turn the headquarters over to the Europeans."

"We going home, sir?" asked Silver.

He smiled. "I have been instructed that AfriKorps is to be redeployed to southeast Asia. I've been selected as the commander of what will be called AsiaKorps!"

"Are you looking for volunteers, Colonel." asked Armbrust.

"I am."

Puhaly stepped forward. "Request permission to accompany the colonel."

"Permission granted."

Armbrust was next. "I'd like to lead Panther squadron for you, sir."

"That you will. Request accepted."

He looked at Creighton. "What about you . . . son?"

Creighton looked at Silver, then at Clayton. "A combat zone is no place to raise a family."

Clayton nodded approvingly. "I think you're right. I've arranged transport for you to the United States within the week."

Creighton laughed. "You knew?"

Clayton pointed at Silver. "Any son of mine who would pick combat over living with that woman and my grandchild would be no son of mine."

Clayton looked at Roman and Shona. "There's always room for the two of you."

Roman shook his head. "I'm staying here . . . with Shona. There's much to teach. Much to learn."

Clayton nodded. "As you wish."

He went to a cabinet and took out a bottle of Aberlour scotch whiskey—the last bottle given him more than a year before by Dr. Carl Eliason. The scotch was with Eliason when he and several hundred others had sealed themselves in a cryogenic pyramid buried in 2055. The colony had ridden out the Cataclysm in their underground frozen tombs.

He poured each person a drink, then raised his glass and toasted:

AfriKorps!

★★★★★★★★★★★★★
Epilogue: DesFor
★★★★★★★

Vegas Biosphere.

To Creighton, the sun in western Nevada seemed smaller than the African sun he had last seen only three months before. In the American desert the efforts of the agronomists since AfriKorps had left in 2175 were showing great signs of productivity.

Cactus was growing, providing habitats for the small creatures now populating the desert south of the biosphere—what was left of it. The biosphere was mostly empty, used now primarily as a research center providing a variety of assistance to the small townships sprouting up in the area. The government had decreed it was safe—and time—to rebuild the country. Like pioneers of the eighteenth and nineteenth centuries, men, women, and children were living on and plowing the land, restocking the lakes and rivers, bringing life back to the land that was so devastated by the Cataclysm.

Creighton walked his plot of land in the mountains where he and Silver had decided to build an earth home. Cool in the summer, solar heated in the winter, it was, he realized, where he would live in peace the rest of his life. Or so he planned.

"I love you," she whispered. He felt her fingers

close around his, and looking at her, noticed how she was getting larger from their expected child.

"What about Reno, and Puhaly?" Silver asked.

Creighton laughed. "They'll be fine."

"Do you have any regrets?"

He shrugged. "There's time when I miss them. And the life. But that's in the past. This is what I've always wanted."

"To be a farmer?"

He bristled. "I'm not a farmer! I'm a rancher."

It was her turn to laugh. "You drive a tractor like you drove your tank—with total abandon. You nearly destroyed our home this morning."

He remembered, and he laughed. "That was funny. I should have had the government agent show me how it works."

"You'll learn. In time."

Time. That was a commodity he now had plenty of. He wasn't responsible for the lives of other people; nor his troops. Only her and the baby that was due in four months.

"There is something you might consider."

"What's that?"

She took a folded sheet of paper and gave it to him. "This came for you this morning."

He read the letter, then looked at her. "What do you think?"

"I think President Dawson has made a wise decision."

"We would have to leave and live in Vegas."

"Vegas is where I grew up. Where we grew up. It's going to be a beautiful city some day. At least, so long as you're not allowed to drive a tractor."

He chuckled. "You have a point. I can't see myself sitting out here on a farm. What do you think?"

"I think you would make a fine governor of Nevada. We needed soldiers, now we need leaders. It's time to rebuild. That means we'll need leaders who understand the price that's been paid for this second chance. So it doesn't happen again. We are the caretakers of this planet. We can't allow the earth to die again. Nature might not give us another chance."

In that moment his decision was made. She was right: Nature would probably not give the people of earth another chance.

He would tell that to the children being born. He would remind their parents. He would make certain that the people around him understood the delicate balance that can be so easily tilted toward catastrophe.

He would tell them we have only one planet, and we must treat her gently!

BILL DOLAN is the pseudonym of an author who lives in North Dakota. He is a Vietnam veteran and has written several previous novels.

Saddle-up to these

THE REGULATOR by *Dale Colter*
Sam Slater, blood brother of the Apache and a cunning bounty-hunter, is out to collect the big price on the heads of the murderous Pauley gang. He'll give them a single choice: surrender and live, or go for your sixgun.

THE REGULATOR—Diablo At Daybreak
by Dale Colter
The Governor wants the blood of the Apache murderers who ravaged his daughter. He gives Sam Slater a choice: work for him, or face a noose. Now Slater must hunt down the deadly renegade Chacon...Slater's Apache brother.

THE JUDGE by *Hank Edwards*
Federal Judge Clay Torn is more than a judge—sometimes he has to be the jury *and* the executioner. Torn pits himself against the most violent and ruthless man in Kansas, a battle whose final verdict will judge one man right...and one man dead.

THE JUDGE—War Clouds
by Hank Edwards
Judge Clay Torn rides into Dakota where the Cheyenne are painting for war and the army is shining steel and loading lead. If war breaks out, someone is going to make a pile of money on a river of blood.

HarperPaperbacks *By Mail*

5 great westerns!

THE RANGER *by Dan Mason*
Texas Ranger Lex Cranshaw is after a killer whose weapon isn't a gun, but a deadly noose. Cranshaw has vowed to stop at nothing to exact justice for the victims, whose numbers are still growing…but the next number up could be his own.

Here are 5 Western adventure tales that are as big as all outdoors! You'll thrill to the action and Western-style justice: swift, exciting, and man-to-man!

Buy 4 or more and save!
When you buy 4 or more books, the postage and handling is FREE!

VISA and MasterCard holders—call 1-800-331-3761 for fastest service!

MAIL TO: Harper Collins Publishers, P. O. Box 588, Dunmore, PA 18512-0588, Tel: (800) 331-3761

YES, send me the Western novels I've checked:
- ☐ **The Regulator** 0-06-100100-7....$3.50
- ☐ **The Regulator/ Diablo At Daybreak** 0-06-100140-6....$3.50
- ☐ **The Judge** 0-06-100072-8 ...$3.50
- ☐ **The Judge/War Clouds** 0-06-100131-7....$3.50
- ☐ **The Ranger** 0-06-100110-4....$3.50

SUBTOTAL .... $_____

POSTAGE AND HANDLING* .... $_____

SALES TAX (NJ, NY, PA residents) .... $_____

Remit in US funds, do not send cash

TOTAL: $_____

Name_____

Address_____

City_____

State_____ Zip_____

Allow up to 6 weeks delivery. Prices subject to change.

*Add $1 postage/handling for up to 3 books…
FREE postage/handling if you buy 4 or more.

H0131

If you enjoyed the Zane Grey book you have just read...

GET THESE 8 GREAT

Harper Paperbacks brings you Zane Grey,

THE RAINBOW TRAIL. Shefford rides a perilous trail to a small stone house near Red Lake, where a new enemy awaits him—and an Indian girl leads him on a dangerous adventure toward Paradise Valley and his explosive destiny.

THE DUDE RANGER. Greenhorn Ernest Selby inherits a sprawling Arizona ranch that's in big trouble. Pitted against the crooked ranch manager and his ruthless band of outlaws, Selby is sure bullets will fly....

THE BORDER LEGION. Roving outlaws led by the notorious Kells kidnap an innocent young bride and hold her in their frightening grasp. Thus begins a wave of crime that could be stopped only by a member of their own vicious legion of death.

THE MAN OF THE FOREST. Milt Dale wanders alone amid the timbered ridges and dark forests of the White Mountains. One night, he stumbles upon a frightening plot that drives him from his beloved wilderness with a dire warning and an inspiring message.

THE LOST WAGON TRAIN. Tough Civil War survivor Stephen Latch will never be the same again. Emerged from the bloodshed a bitter man, a brigand with a ready gun, he joins a raging Indian chief on a mission of terrifying revenge—to massacre a pioneer train of 160 wagons. But fate has a big surprise!

WILDFIRE. Wildfire is a legend, a fiery red stallion who is captured and broken by horse trainer Lin Stone. A glorious beast, a miracle, Wildfire is also a curse—a horse who could run like the wind and who could also spill the blood of those who love him most.

HarperPaperbacks By Mail

ZANE GREY WESTERNS

the greatest chronicler of the American West!

SUNSET PASS. Six years ago Trueman Rock killed a man in Wagontongue. Now he's back and in trouble again. But this time it's the whole valley's trouble—killing trouble—and only Rock's blazing six-gun can stop it.

30,000 ON THE HOOF. Logan Huett, former scout for General Crook on his campaign into Apache territory, carries his innocent new bride off to a life in a lonely canyon where human and animal predators threaten his dream of raising a strong family and a magnificent herd.

Zane Grey is a true legend. His best selling novels have thrilled generations of readers with heart-and guts characters, hard shooting action, and high-plains panoramas. Zane Grey is the genuine article, the real spirit of the Old West.

Buy 4 or More and $ave

When you buy 4 or more books from Harper Paperbacks, the Postage and Handling is **FREE**.

MAIL TO: **Harper Collins Publishers**
P. O. Box 588, Dunmore, PA 18512-0588
Telephone: (800) 331-3761
Visa and MasterCard holders—call
1-800-331-3761 for fastest service!

Yes, please send me the Zane Grey Western adventures I have checked:

- ☐ The Rainbow Trail (0-06-100080-9) $3.50
- ☐ The Dude Ranger (0-06-100055-8) $3.50
- ☐ The Lost Wagon Train (0-06-100064-7) $3.50
- ☐ Wildfire (0-06-100081-7) $3.50
- ☐ The Man Of The Forest (0-06-100082-5) $3.50
- ☐ The Border Legion (0-06-100083-3) $3.50
- ☐ Sunset Pass (0-06-100084-1) $3.50
- ☐ 30,000 On The Hoof (0-06-100085-X) $3.50

SUBTOTAL .... $_____

POSTAGE AND HANDLING* .... $_____

SALES TAX (NJ, NY, PA residents) .... $_____

TOTAL: $_____
(Remit in US funds, do not send cash.)

Name_____

Address_____

City_____

State_____ Zip_____ Allow up to 6 weeks delivery. Prices subject to change.

*Add $1 postage/handling for up to 3 books…
FREE postage/handling if you buy 4 or more.

H0011